the Wife

the Wife

Rosmini Shaari

Translated by

Normala Othman

Make-Do Publishing (UK), Third Floor, 207 Regents Street, London W1B 3HH., UK
Make-Do Publishing (Asia), 19th Floor, 262 Des Voeux Road Central, Hong Kong

First published in Malay as Isteri.
© Rosmini Shaari 1988
Translation © Normala Othman
This book was published with support from Institut Terjemahan Negara Malaysia Berhad. This edition published in 2015 by Fortysix Books, an imprint of Make-Do Publishing.

Cover design by Mugdha Sadhwani
Printed and bound by
CPI Group (UK) Ltd, Croydon, CR0 4YY.

ISBN 978-988-16775-0-1

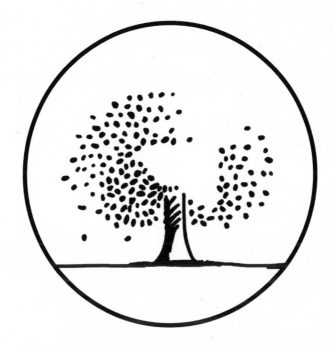

I am baffled by the attitude of human beings who only
pretend to be in love.

1

'IS it true that you're in love with my husband?', Sofia asked nervously.

The café was noisy today. For some reason Nora hadn't anticipated this question. She looked away.

Sofia waited as she stared at the woman who wanted to steal her husband.

'Please be frank,' said Sofia. 'I know you never thought that I would want to see you and I'm grateful that you're willing to come and meet me here.'

'I've come because I need the truth,' said Nora. 'I knew that Halim's wife was called Sofia but that's all. I didn't know anything else. I must confess though: when you called asking to see me, I thought it would be about something more urgent.'

'You think that my question is not urgent...not important? Halim is my husband. Whether you love him is certainly of great importance to me, though perhaps not to you. You're probably in love with many men.'

Nora felt angry but she stayed silent because she didn't know what to say. Her feelings were a personal matter. There was no point in discussing them with others. Nora pressed her lips to the rim of her lychee drink and felt the cold perfumed juice flowing down her throat. So this was Halim's wife. The woman was tall with a fair complexion but a heavy set body.

Sofia bit her tongue. A large part of her wanted to scream and curse but she wasn't going to behave like an ignorant person. She only wanted an explanation from the young woman facing her. 'You haven't answered my question,' she said impatiently.

'Yes, I know...'

'So, how about it?'

'Why do you want to know how I feel?' asked Nora.

'Alright, if you want to hear my explanation, I will explain. But after I've stated the truth, I will expect you to state your feelings,' Sofia said.

Nora felt nervous confronting a woman as direct as this. She'd expected a gentler, softer woman who would utter curses accompanied by tears. Sofia seemed calm and clear-headed.

'Look Nora, I prefer things to be simple. Life is just life with all its challenges, not more than that. I accept everything that happens in my life fully and patiently. If Halim no longer loves me, I will not beg or force him. He is free with his feelings. What I want in my life is the truth. I don't like to live in limbo. I don't want to convince myself that my husband still loves me, when he does not. I don't want to live in mere fantasy.'

'What would you do if I told you the truth?' asked Nora.

'That will not be your responsibility,' said Sofia. 'Furthermore, we have an agreement and now that I've stated my feelings and wishes, it's your turn to be frank. Answer honestly and sincerely. Imagine that I am not Halim's wife.'

Nora nodded slowly. 'If that is so, alright. What would you like to know?'

'What is your relationship with Halim?'

2

'We are quite close. I don't believe that anyone is at fault in this matter.'

'What do you mean?' Sofia was trying to stay calm but her heart was heating up.

'Halim is a handsome and attractive man.'

'Yes he is' said Sofia, 'but you still have not answered my question. Are you in love with my husband?'

'I am still not sure if it is love. I know I'm attracted to Halim. But, I still don't believe in love.' Nora stopped and bit her thumb.

'I suppose you've had your heart broken before?' asked Sofia.

'Yes.' Nora looked down for a moment. There was a bitterness in her face. How foolish she'd been. She'd never thought that the man of her choice would break his promise to her. She shook her head and quickly wiped away the memory.

'How about Halim?' asked Sofia. 'Does he love you?'

'Why don't you ask him yourself?'

'He's not aware that I know of your relationship with him. He is still acting like the ideal husband deeply in love with his wife.'

'Oh...' Nora felt offended by these words.

'Would you like another drink? Waiter! Please bring another glass of mango juice and....'

'One lychee.'

Sofia turned back to Nora. 'Are you free this afternoon?'

'Yes, I'm free.' She stared at Sofia. 'He really doesn't know that you know about me?'

Sofia nodded.

'How did you find out?'

'I heard him calling you one night...'

'Oh....'

Sofia's thoughts always dwelled on that night. Halim was working late in his study and thought she was asleep. Sofia lifted the telephone receiver to call her mother and then overheard Halim's conversation with Nora. As she'd listened she could feel her heart breaking up into hundred of tiny pieces. Later she obtained more evidence from her friends.

'What are you going to do now?' asked Nora.

The woman was truly brave to ask such a question, thought Sofia.

'That depends on you. What is your aim? What is your hope? Is your relationship with Halim serious, or is this just a game for you? If it's only a short-term thing, I'm willing to wait until Halim is bored with you. If you want it to continue, I need to discuss things with Halim,' said Sofia.

Nora started. It was not possible for Halim to be bored with her. Halim loved her with all his heart.'So you believe that Halim will leave me one day?' she said.

'Well ... what is so special about any woman? I was young once like you. My body used to be more attractive than it is now. If he can leave me because he is crazy for you ... one day he will also leave you because you are no longer young. You are getting older too, you know. You are catching me up.'

Nora was about to get angry but stopped herself when a waiter brought two glasses, placed them on the table and then left.

Nora had never expected that Sofia, who she had always imagined as gentle, was capable of such words. There was some truth to what Sofia had just said.

'That is why I want to know the real situation, whether you love Halim or not. If you love him, that's alright. Surely you

4

can sacrifice your future for happiness today. Isn't that what love means? Love requires sacrifice. There is no love if there is no sacrifice. If you really love Halim, you will do anything as long as you can keep his love. You will sacrifice your future happiness.' Sofia was trembling but she felt calmer now tshe had poured out everything that she had been keeping inside.

The tears began to well in Nora's eyes. It was impossible that Halim would do such a thing, impossible! Suddenly she stood up and grabbed her handbag. 'Never!' she yelled at Sofia. 'Never! Never!' She turned and ran.

The other customers were staring but Sofia ignored them. She did not move from her seat but concentrated on drinking slowly the mango juice she had ordered. She never looked round and she paid no attention to anything around her.

Driving away, Nora could not stop her tears. Was Sofia right? Was she? And what about Halim? He had often proven his love to her but now, all of a sudden, she was afraid to face the future.

Sofia... Sofia ... are her words true? Are they? I think Sofia has a heart of stone, she is emotionless; yes, she's cruel, Sofia ... she ... she's cruel!

The car stopped. The traffic light, red ... yellow ... green. The car moved again. Nora had no idea where to go. She did not want to go home. Her roommate Asmah would surely notice the tears. She did not want Asmah to know she had been crying. She did not want to be grilled about her tears. A picture of Halim's handsome face came into her mind. Oh, Halim!

She thought about the first time they met. She had been driving and her car had broken down at the bend near the main road. While she was opening the bonnet another car had stopped beside her. The driver who got out was of average height with a handsome face. 'Miss, what's wrong with your car?'

'I don't know, the engine won't start,' Nora eyed the stranger apprehensively.

'Miss, you are going to the office, is that right? I believe we work in the same building.'

Nora nodded.

'OK, come, I'll take you ... save you being late!'

They pushed her car to the roadside. Nora locked the doors and quickly climbed into the front seat of the man's car.

'My name is Halim, what about you, miss?'

'Nora,' she said.

'Leave the car here first, go to the office, later on you can come back,' said Halim.

'It'll be difficult to find a mechanic from the office...'

'If so, I can come back to look at your car later. Miss, write down your telephone number. When I have the time I'll call you. After that we can come back to the car....'

Oh Halim, thought Nora. She'd never thought that someone so courteous would behave in the way described by Sofia earlier.

Nora had been attracted to Halim from that first day they met and she believed that he had never lied to her. He apppeared honest and sincere, telling her everything about his wife and children. Nora was actually disappointed about that, because if he'd said nothing they might have had a more intimate relationship. But Halim was an honest husband and a loving father.

Since then they'd met often. It wasn't difficult: they worked

6

in the same building.

Oh, Halim! I do not believe Sofia. She is a cruel woman. Halim is not like that.

Nora stopped by the roadside and turned off the engine. The road was quiet with vehicles seldom passing by. She looked up at the clouds parading slowly. Golden yellow was beginning to thread the twilight sky. What should I do now? Why do I have doubts? Is it possible that I truly love Halim? Could this be the love I had been looking for all my life?

But if Halim really behaved as described by Sofia, I would surely suffer terribly.

The car engine was turned on again. Nora drove toward her house unable to decide whether or not to tell Halim about her meeting with Sofia.

When Sofia got home, she found that Halim had not returned from golf. The house was empty and quiet. Her soul was empty but her heart was aching. What should she do? How should she act? All she knew was that Nora had succeeded in attracting Halim.

Sofia gazed at the fast-spinning ceiling fan. She did not want to blame herself. Up to that point she had worked hard to be a good and considerate wife. She touched her face. Sofia was aware that her looks could still attract other men. She knew that if she wanted she could also have opportunities to cheat, but that was not the way to take her revenge. She wasn't insane. She should do something mature. She could fight fire with fire but what she really needed was water to cure and cool down the blaze.

In the silence of the empty house, the music from her neighbour's organ could be heard. Often those sad songs would haunt Sofia when she was alone. In earlier times, when her children, Amin and Hasni, were still small, they would fill the loneliness but now they were all grown up, each had left to further their studies. Sofia had lived her entire life for her family's happines. If Halim wanted to destroy all of that then Sofia would not sit still. She would not allow her marriage, which she had been happy for so long, to fall apart so easily.

'What happened?' asked Asmah, closing the door. Her voice was heavy with curiosity.

Nora was sitting on the bed. Traces of tears could still be seen in her eyes. She was still.

'You had a fight with her?' asked Asmah again. 'She hit you perhaps? I told you not to go, but you still went. That's why ... you don't want to listen to me! Now who's suffering?'

Nora said nothing. She studied the end of the handkerchief, which she was holding tightly in her hand. Asmah perched on the edge of the bed and touched Nora's shoulder. 'As I mentioned earlier, don't be friendly with other people's husbands. You said that you could take care of yourself. Why are you crying now?'

Nora began to sob.

'Nora, why don't you tell me what really happened. His wife was angry with you?'

Finally Nora looked up. 'No Asmah, she wasn't angry. She didn't even feel anything. I've never met a more stone-hearted woman. Perhaps she is without feelings.'

'So why are you crying? There must be something that's causing you to cry. She must have surely cursed you,' said Asmah again. 'If someone stole my husband, I wouldn't just curse her, I wouldl beat her up. Well, I already told you not to be too close with Halim!' Asmah knew she was nagging but she could not help herself. Nora wouldn't tell her anything unless she nagged.

'Yes, I know you meant well. I tried to distance myself. But....'

'But now you are upset because his wife picked on you.'

'It's not about that. She wasn't even angry. She only wanted to know my position and my feelings.'

'And then?' Asmah was impatient. 'So, you told her the truth?'

'Not all of it. I only gave her some indication, but she understood alright. What makes me sad is that she said one day Halim would probably leave me if he met another woman who was younger, more attractive. He would have wasted my life.'

Asmah was quiet.

'What do you think, Asmah? What should I do?'

'I've already advised you and you don't want to listen to me. Now only when you are stuck, you cry!'

'Yes, I know I'm wrong but what could I do? This is all fate, don't you see?'

'A fate that you sought,' said Asmah, folding her arms.

'That's also true, I got close to him, but he is handsome. I become weak if the man is handsome, I can't can't top looking at him.'

'If only it was only looking!' said Asmah. 'First, it is looking, then touching—that's why I told you not to be alone with him.'

'Don't be like that Asmah.' Nora began to laugh.

'Forget it, what is there to worry about? His wife wasn't even angry with you. All she's done is ask about your feelings for her husband.'

'Yes, but the question now is will Halim behave in the way described by his wife? Will he leave me one day?'

'Eh ... eh, what's wrong with you? You said yourself that it wasn't serious, it was only a casual romance. You said you wanted to use all men because all men are bastards!' Asmah's voice was becoming agitated.

Nora fell silent: she realized that the trap she had been setting all this time had finally ensnared her. After a while she spoke again. 'Before I met Halim's wife I didn't understand what was happening with Halim. I realize now that I love him. But Halim's wife thinks that he'll leave me when he gets bored and meets another pretty woman. She says I have to sacrifice my future in order to be with Hallim.'

'And you aren't willing to make that sacrifice?'

'His wife says that love requires sacrifice. If I truly loved Halim I would surely be willing to face all problems,' said Nora.

'So?' Asmah was perplexed.

'So, right now I cannot think. I realize that I love him, but I am afraid that what his wife has said might come true.'

'But love, Nora? I remember when you told me it was revenge you wanted; that you were angry with all men because your ex-lover married another woman.'

'Yes, I know, that's what I'm saying. Perhaps if I stay with Halim I will end up as the trapped one after all.'

Asmah frowned. 'Who knows, Halim himself might not be in love with you. I don't trust men. After my father took another wife, I gave up wanting to marry. I know how my mother suffered. Well, I cannot describe how I cried everyday.'

Nora appeared not to be listening to Asmah. 'I don't want to give up. Once, I allowed my lover to be snatched by someone else. Now times have changed. If I really want someone, I won't stop half way.'

'What happened to your trap?'

'My trap has turned into a castle that is giving happiness to me and Halim.'

'What about his wife?'

'His wife? That is not my problem. His wife said so herself. It is her own problem. My problem is how to take care of Halim so the castle that we built is not destroyed in the storm.'

Norah looked pleased all of a sudden but anxiety crept over Asmah's heart. She began to think about her mother who had suffered because she had to share her husband with another woman. People who behaved like Nora made Asmah fear marriage.

Suddenly, she felt hatred for her close friend.

2

HALIM was busy at his writing desk when there was a knock at the door. Who would want to see him this early in the morning? The knock came again. He needed to finish his work before ten that morning.

'Come in,' said Halim, not looking up at who had entered. His mind was on his work. 'Sit down...,' he continued with his eyes focused on the paper in front of him and his pen still dancing non-stop.

There was silence for a moment and then Halim looked up, puzzled. He stared at the person standing stiffly in front of him and his pen stopped dancing. A smile formed on Halim's lips. 'Wati! Is it really Wati?'

'Yes, it is Wati! Who else would it be? I thought you would have forgotten my name.' Fatimawati was standing in front of him smiling sweetly.

'Eh never, please sit down!'

Wati had not changed, she was still stylish as before, still as slim, still as attractive. Perhaps only her outfit was different. She was wearing a long grey skirt and a pink blouse.

'It's been a while since we met,' she said, adjusting the scarf at her neck.

'Yes, almost a quarter of a decade.'

'Eh, don't count how long it has been. I don't want to feel that old.' Wati smiled now.

'You can never be old, I can see that you've not changed one bit from then till now.' Halim pressed the bell near his right hand and a moment later an office boy knocked on the door and entered.

'Ahmad, please bring some drinks. Wati, what would you like to drink?'

'Coffee, without sugar and milk.'

'Eh, trying to slim down? Don't be too thin or else you'll lose your guitar shape,' said Halim, smiling.

'I fear that I might become the shape of a drum,' said Wati. Both of them laughed.

'Alright then, two coffees, one without sugar and milk, the other one with sugar and milk,' Halim said to Ahmad, who was busy looking at Wati.

'Yes, sir,' said Ahmad as he walked out.

'Since when have you been paying attention to your body?' asked Halim.

'The Japanese control what they eat. Think about it Halim, none of them are fat, all of them are thin. Their old men are also handsome. Every morning, they walk.'

'When did you go to Japan?'

'I just returned from there. I was on a six-month course.'

'So where do you work now?'

'Here.'

'Which office?'

'This office!'

'Eh, I don't believe you!' said Halim. 'How is it that I didn't know?'

'Ah, you're busy with meetings here and conferences there, how would you know what's happening in your own office?'

'Eh ... hh, it's not possible! Not possible.' Halim was

puzzled. 'But it's true. I knew there was someone coming to replace Mr Jaafar, but I didn't know it was you.'

'Yes, everything was at the last minute, I myself did not expect it.'

'So, you started today?'

'Yes, that's right.'

Halim shook his head in disbelief. 'And what happened to your boyfriend, the one you were seeing back in University? Did you marry him?'

'Which one?'

'OK, come on, I ... see, that's what happens when you have too many boyfriends!' Halim smiled.

'No, really. I can't remember which one you mean.'

'The one with the red sports car!'

'Eh, no, that's Datuk Dollah's son. Ah, he's a true Romeo! At least he thought he was Romeo...' Her brow wrinkled. 'Can women be *Romeo* too?'

'*Juliet*....' Halim corrected her.

There was a knock on the door and Ahmad entered with drinks. He placed them on the table, glancing at Wati from the corner of his eyes.

After he'd left, Halim leaned back in his chair.'So, who did you marry?'

'I didn't meet him at the university, but at a school far away from town.'

'You used to teach?'

'Eh, as if you didn't know!'

'So where's your husband now?'

'He's still in Kampung Kaloi.'

'Kampung Kaloi?' Halim was puzzled.

'Have you heard of the name Rahim Ahmad from Kaloi?'

14

'Oh, the Honourable Rahim Ahmad?'

'Yes.'

'That's your husband?' Halim was confused. 'Oh yes, he used to be a teacher, after that he got involved in politics!'

'Yes.'

'Please, have some coffee,' said Halim

'Thank you.' Wati lifted the cup and straight away took a sip.

'Where do you stay?' asked Halim, as he reached for his cup at the table.

'Here,' answered Wati, 'in the city, with two other friends.'

'Your son?'

'My son, Hisham, is in a boarding school in Kuala Kangsar.'

'Hm ... one there, one here....' Halim was even more puzzled.

'How about you? Who's your wife? Did you marry that girl, Nita?'

'No ... my wife is from my hometown. She's not working.'

'Yes, it's better to stay at home. What's her name?'

'Sofia.'

The telephone on the desk rang.

'Hello, this is Halim, yes...? Oh yes, Fatimawati, yes, she's here. O.K. I'll ask her to go there. O.K. Bye.'

He replaced the receiver.

'Wati ... you're wanted in the boss' office.'

'O.K., I'll go now.' Wati got up, and reached for her handbag.

'Wati ...'

She turned around.

'I'd like to invite you to my house. I'll fix the day later,' said Halim.

'O.K., thank you,' Wati said and left.

Nora ran into Ahmad while the latter was leaving Halim's office. Ahmad smiled coyly to imply he knew something.

'Miss Nora would like to see Mr Halim?'

'Yes,' replied Nora, puzzled, 'why are you smiling?'

'He had a special guest this morning!' said Ahmad, trying to goad her on.

'Who was it?' Nora was curious. Rogayah, who was sitting at the desk next to where Nora was standing, was also smiling, but her eyes were on the paper she was typing.

'I don't know. Mr Halim called her, Wati. A very attractive person, with a guitar-shaped body, sir said.' Ahmad smiled again.

'Mr Halim said that?' Nora was beginning to feel worried. Jealousy crept into her heart.

'Hmm, she was really gorgeous.' Ahmad rubbed his chest. If you want to see her, go ahead.'

Rogayah continued to smile and could not focus on her task. She wanted to see Nora's reaction. What would she do? Nora looked uncertain. She went directly to Aminah's desk and Aminah pretended not to hear anything that had happened.

Ahmad looked at Rogayah. Rogayah smiled and Ahmad thought it was funny.

'Minah, who's in Halim's office?' asked Nora.

'Her name is Fatimawati. She's one of the new managers,' answered Aminah. 'Do you want to see Mr Halim?'

'Yes,' said Nora, holding on to the edge of Aminah's desk.

'Even if you see them now, Mr Halim will not be angry. They're just talking.'

'Oii! It's his ex-girlfriend, you know!' Ahmad whispered loudly.

'Is that true?' Nora asked Aminah slowly, afraid that Rogayah might hear. Nora was beginning to have doubts. She remembered Sofia's words the afternoon before. But she calmed herself. She did not want to admit defeat. Both managers? Not very likely! Both of them at the same level! Malaysian men do not like women who are of the same level as them. Nora's chances were still bright!

'Would you like to see Mr Halim now?' asked Aminah again, 'I can call him.'

'Don't, I don't want to spoil their programme. I want to see how long they talk,' said Nora.

'Well, you sound jealous!' said Aminah.

'Ah you just can't stop. You know me full well. I can get guys better than Halim, if I want to.'

'Won't your boss be angry if you wait around here all day?'

'He's overseas.'

The telephone in front of Aminah rang. 'Good morning… yes… I'll connect you now,' she said.

'Who's that?' asked Nora.

'Mr Majid…,'

'Eh, is that person really gorgeous?' Nora was still thinking about Wati.

'He has a paunch, bald head.'

'Who are you talking about?'

'Eh, who are you asking about? Mr Majid, right?'

'No! I'm asking about his ex-girlfriend inside there!'

17

Before Aminah could say anything, Wati came out from Halim's room. Nora stared at her, heart pounding. Long curly hair, curled eye lashes...

'If you'd like to go right in,' said Aminah.

Nora was still uncertain.

'Well, what's there to be afraid of? Fatimawati's married and also has a child,' said Aminah.

Nora's face became cheerful again. She's already married. I'm still young and beautiful. She recalled Sofia's words. Ah, forget it, Sofia was probably trying to scare her.

Nora smiled.

'Alright, I'll see you later,' said Nora to Aminah. She approached Halim's room.

Aminah found the situation truly hilarious. She turned towards Rogayah. Rogayah jeered.

'Why did you tell her so soon?' said Rogayah. 'It would have been funnier if she did not know. I wanted to see what she would do. There could have been a big scene in there.'

'I don't know, Rogayah, it's difficult for me to do my job if she's always here disturbing me. The sooner I tell her, the sooner I can get on with things.'

'Doesn't she have any work to do?'

'I don't know, I don't want to know about other people's matters. If I could finish my work every day, that would be a relief.'

'Yes, I'm also feeling the same, but you're right: it's quite difficult if people like that come and disturb us without any reason,' said Rogayah.

'Ah, but that's also our responsibility, we have to entertain them, no matter who comes.'

Ahmad appeared again, rushing into the office.

'Eh, Ahmad, what's happened, you look breathless!' said Rogayah.

'Ooi, driving a BM ... W white ... e ... ee ... e what else does she want? A BMW!!' Ahmad snapped his fingers as he turned his body gleefully.

'Hey, whose BMW?' asked Rogayah.

'Who else, but Miss Wati,' said Ahmad.

'Eh, her husband is the Honourable Gentleman? Naturally it would be a BMW. Even if it was a Mercedes sportscar, she could afford it,' said Aminah, but her eyes were fixed on the paper in front of her.

'She's the wife of the Honourable Gentleman?' asked Ahmad, surprised, his eyes bulging.

'Ah, that's enough Ahmad ... get to work. We are trying to work here, you are always talking about other people's business, poking your nose into other people's affairs, so to speak.'

'Business, not affairs!' Ahmad grinned as he left the office.

'Hmm, if Ahmad wasn't here for a day, things would be pretty quiet,' said Aminah,laughing.

'Yes, that's true.'

Rogayah joined in the laughter but both of them stopped when they saw Nora rushing out of Halim's office. Her face was red.

They could hear Halim's voice calling Nora to come back. Nora showed her fury by ignoring him. Rogayah and Aminah looked at each other. They did not say a word. But they sensed that a volcano was about to erupt.

The telephone rang while Sofia was still putting on her lipstick. She hurriedly left her room and went directly to the telephone console that was near the TV area.

'Hello.'

'Sofia, where were you yesterday afternoon? I called but you weren't in.'

'Rahmah! What's wrong?'

'Nothing, I hear there's a sale in town. I want to know if you'd like to come along.'

'Hmm ... ah ... I'm not in the mood today.'

'What's wrong with you, are you ill?'

'N ... no, I'm not ill.'

'Then, why do I hear something is not quite right in your voice?'

'I don't know Rahmah, I feel empty all of a sudden.'

'Something must be wrong,' said Rahmah, concerned. 'Don't think too much. *If you follow your heart you'll die, if you follow your feelings, you'll be destroyed.*'

'Die or destroyed, what's the difference?'

'Something must have happened.'

'Yes....' Sofia recalled the meeting the previous afternoon.

'Where were you yesterday afternoon? In the morning you were alright, when I called you about what to buy at the market. Yes, you were out yesterday afternoon. I called everywhere, but could not reach you.'

'Hmm....'

'What's this ... yes ... hmm ... yes ... hmm ... you have not answered any of my questions.'

'I don't know Rahmah, I've given up hope.'

'In what?'

'In everything.'

Rahmah tutted. 'Are you trying to hide something from me? You want to keep it a secret? If you don't tell anyone how you feel, you will surely feel worse. If you let it all out, you will feel much better.'

'I just... I feel defeated, I feel crushed. I feel like the sky is falling in on me. I feel like I'm suffocating.'

'I can come over to your house if you like.'

'Don't trouble yourself, thank you,' said Sofia. 'It's not that I don't want you to come. Jo would surely have come home for tea by then, it is better that you wait for him.'

'Sofia, if you are troubled, I will also feel troubled. Please don't think that you're alone in the world. I want to help you.'

'Yes, I know Rahmah. But this is my own troublee. I think I'm now mature enough to handle my trouble without troubling others.'

'Alright, if you think so. I don't want to push you. But do remember, anytime you want someone to talk to, I am here. Just call me, I will come over.'

'Thank you Rahmah, talking with you makes me feel better. Halim is home, I can hear his car. We'll see each other later, O.K. Thank you!'

The telephone was replaced; Sofia went to the door. She knew Halim had his own key, but it had become her habit to welcome home her husband and she didn't want him to know that anything had changed. Halim was not going to find out yet that Sofia knew about the affair.

'What's wrong Sofia? You look down. It is somewhat gloomy

today,' said Halim.

Sofia tried to respond, but she was not a good actor. If her heart was bitter, her face was also morose. Her smile was forced. 'Ah, nothing's wrong. Would you like to have tea now?'

'No, later. I'd like to sit down for a while. Could you massage my neck a little. I feel rather exhausted.'

Sofia went to Halim who was sitting on the sofa. She massaged Halim's neck without saying anything.

'Sofia, were you working so hard today that you're too tired to say a word?'

'I don't know, I don't feel well.' Sofia had never lied before, but she did not want to say what was really in her mind. She felt the world was becoming darker.

Halim turned to look at Sofia.

'Eh, I think it's best if we go to the doctor. You never know – it might be something serious.'

Sofia shook her head. 'I just need some rest, I'll be alright.'

'Perhaps you're fed-up, staying at home alone in the house? Hasni and Amin used to be here, but now they're grown up. They have their own lives.'

'Yes, that's what I was thinking about. Perhaps it's time for us to separate. Perhaps I should think about my own future. I'm wondering what will happen if I have to face life alone.'

'What are you saying Sofia?' Halim was puzzled. He was worried.

'For some reason, I feel the loneliness has become more intense ever since Hasni and Amin left.' Quickly, she tried to change the subject, so that Halim would not become suspicious.

'You're feeling lonely, aren't you, Sofia? Poor you. What

can we do? I am always so busy with work... Why don't you ask mother to come and live here. There would always be someone to talk to then.'

'Mother doesn't want to come, she has her chickens and ducks. They could not just be left alone even for a little while. Old folks, wherever they go, their minds will still be in their village.'

The telephone rang. Sofia got up leaving Halim on the sofa. She lifted the receiver.

'Hello? Yes, he's here ... Halim, telephone!'

Sofia went through to the kitchen. She knew it was Ramli on the telephone. There would surely be something planned. Nevertheless, Sofia reheated the food that she had cooked earlier.

'Sofia!' She heard Halim calling. 'Ramli called. He asked me to go with him to Datuk Kassim's house; I have no idea what he wants to discuss there.'

'Won't you eat first?'

'I think we'll just eat out,' he said.

'Hmm, alright,' said Sofia.

Reluctantly, Halim went to change before meeting Ramli. He knew that Sofia was not too happy with him dining out that evening. She was lonely and wanted company.

Sofia watched him leave the room. She knew she would be alone that night. She missed her children and her mother, who were far away. Sadness choked her.

After Halim drove away, Sofia stood by the open gates, looking out on to the road. She began thinking again about the strange meeting yesterday and as she thought, she began to pace until, without realizing it, Sofia had walked right through the gates and out on to the road. Outside, the breeze cooled Sofia's heart. She truly liked to take a walk in the area around Selasih Road. She knew the door to her house was not locked, but she did not let it bother her because she was only going out for a short while. She looked at the darkening sky. From far away she could hear the faint rhythm of a sad song and the mournful music cut into Sofia's soul. She knew those heartbreaking songs came from the white house, number 1912. They could often be heard particularly on lonely nights like this. Often, the songs entertained Sofia while she was alone, without her children and husband.

Sofia began to think about herself. Her children were grown up. Her husband was of a high position, and stable in his job. What else could I ask for? Each time after prayer, I would ask for my family's success, for their happiness. Thank God, they are all well. Why should I worry anymore? That is what I have prayed for all this while, that is what I have hoped for.

But why do I feel anxious beyond words? Why is my life lonely, meaningless?

If the loneliness and worry in my life could eventually give me happiness, I would be willing to be lonely, I would be willing to have this anxiety in my heart, burning in my chest.

Why must women be softhearted? Why are women gentle, jealous without reason?

For now, my marriage is quiet. But happy? I don't know! Perhaps Halim is happy, but me ... physically I'm suffering and spiritually I'm weak. I'm like a shadow that comes and goes, that disappears and reappears.

The songs heard in the distance were getting louder. Sofia

knew she was approaching house number 1912. There used to be two cars parked here, a white Volvo and a yellow Honda. Now there was only the white Volvo. Each time Sofia passed by there, the place looked desolate. During the day, it was empty without any trace of human beings and now she wondered why. Sofia had never met the occupants. Living in a such a big city, neighbours hardly knew each other. The only thing Sofia knew was that the beguiling songs disturbed her soul. The only thing Sofia knew was that the songs deepened the sorrow in her heart. She returned home. She was slightly worried that her house was not locked. The songs could be heard faintly. Sofia's mind was truly anxious.

3

THE house of Halim and Sofia was situated in a locality quite far from the city. It had been Halim's long time wish to build a home in a quiet and peaceful area, and he had worked hard to achieve his dream. He also believed that Sofia was happy with the house that he had chosen. If Sofia was happy, Halim felt relieved because Sofia was the one who had to stay home all day long. Halim was there only a few hours a day.

Halim wandered into the kitchen where Sofia was still busy preparing tea.

'Sofia!'

'Yes?' Sofia turned to Halim who stood at the kitchen door looking dashing in a red sports jacket. Halim was always handsome, Sofia thought. She smiled at him.

'Do you need help?' asked Halim.

'Ah, no, everything is ready. Are all the guests here?'

'Not yet.'

'Hmm, take the refreshments outside first, if anybody else comes, we'll make some more.'

'O.K. Eh, if you are done, come out, I'd like to introduce you to my friends.'

'Alright,' Sofia adjusted her hair. Seeing Halim being so attentive made it almost impossible for Sofia to believe that he was having an affair with another woman.

From outside came the sound of car doors closing and Halim's voice inviting the guests in. Sofia hurried out of the kicthen.

'Sofia, our guests have arrived ... eh, where is the other one?' Halim asked.

'Ah, you obviously have forgotten my name!' one guest joked.

Sofia approached Halim and he placed his hand on her waist.

'Sofia, this is Fatimawati who has just returned from Japan. She was just transferred to my office. We were at university together.'

Fatimawati shook Sofia's hand tightly and the two stared at each other in disbelief.

'Wati!' screamed Sofia. 'Is it really you, Wati?'

Before Wati could reply, they were already hugging each other and laughing.

'Yes, Sofia, it's me,' Wati whispered in Sofia's ear.

Tears started in Sofia's eyes. 'I never thought... it's been years since we met... I thought I'd never see you again...'

Halim was stunned and puzzled; the other guests exchanged confused glances.

'Sofia, do you really know Wati?' asked Halim.

'Wati was my roommate in our school dormitory. We were like flesh and blood, could not be separated from each other.'

'Hmm, I never thought that you two knew each other.'

'Yes, I never thought we would see each other again. Eh, where's your husband?'

'Ah, one can never trust him ... busy all the time.' They were still standing in the yard of Sofia's house.

'Wati's husband is the Honourable Rahim Ahmad, the

People's Representative of Kaloi,' said Halim.

'Oh yes, the new People's Representative, replacing Mr Salleh Hashim? Yes, I remember. Eh, such a coincidence!' said Sofia. She turned again to Wati.

'Please come in,' said Halim.

After dinner the guests split into groups. Datuk Arif, Salman, Ramli and Johari played cards with Halim. A few others discussed politics. Datin Jamilah, Rahmah and Zabidah talked about cooking.

Sofia watched Wati's face lit up by the fire that was roasting the satay in front of them. She was still beautiful as before, and appeared not to have changed one bit. If someone had said she was still young and single, it would have been believable. Her hair was as long as before. At school she had worn it in two plaits but now her hair hung loose to her waist. She was tall and slim.

'Why are you silent, Sofia?' asked Wati as she adjusted herself on the soft grass.

'I was just thinking that you have hardly changed; still attractive, still beautiful like before,' Sofia said, fanning the embers of the fire.

'Sofia, I don't want to think about my age. For me, I am always 26 years old. You surely know my age, but I don't want to know. What do we get from always thinking about how old we are? Everyone, not just you and me, will age. Everyone will become older. If everyone feared getting older, surely there would not be any happy person left on earth. But if you think about it, there's nothing to be afraid of. It's not only us who are getting older, everyone is. Our husbands are not getting younger, they're getting older, just like us,' said Wati.

'Yes but for men, being old is different. As women age they get closer to God, but men, as they become older they become more boyish, looking for girls.'

'Hmmm, I don't care about that. Whatever Rahim wants to do—let him do it. I am here, Rahim stays in Kaloi. Every week Rahim comes over to my place, it's not too far, only twenty miles. He wants to be with "his people," let him. I also have my work. There's no way I'm going to drive everyday to Kaloi. It's a long road. There's also a lot of work at the office. Furthermore, I want to go back to study.'

'Honestly? But what else do you want to study? Isn't the degree that you have enough?'

Wati turned the satay that was nearly cooked. 'Ah that's only a degree, this is different! I will not feel satisfied if I don't pursue a PhD. My studies will be incomplete.'

'Ah you are such an extremist.'

'That's the way it is.'

Sofia smiled at her. 'Wati, how did you end up marrying the Honourable Rahim?'

'Oh, he used to be just a teacher in Kampung Kaloi…'

'And you are a graduate teacher!'

'That's not what I meant.'

'How did you meet him?'

'I don't know, it was meant to be,' said Wati. 'You know how it is in the village. Plus, all new teachers are assigned to the rural areas. I had to go as well and lived in a small house, without piped water. Fortunately, there was Rahim, otherwise, there was nothing in the village to entertain me. He was a quiet person. At first, he was afraid to approach me—well, I was a graduate teacher after all. I placed plenty of traps, but none snared him.'

'You hadn't changed. Never without your tricks,' said Sofia.

'Huh, like you were any different. If we don't have fun while we are still young then, when? It's all about living life to the fullest.'

'So you managed to trap Rahim?'

'I knew he liked me, only he was a little bit nervous.'

'Wati. Who did not like you? All the young men were crazy over you then.'

'How about you? Where did you meet Halim?'

'We've known each other since we were children studying the Qur'an in our village. While I was at school, we wrote letters, many letters but after that we did not see each other for a long time, until he left university. We met again at a friend's wedding in the village. Then we married.'

'Halim was on the same programme as mine, but we didn't get the opportunity to know each other well,' said Wati as she lifted the satay that was almost burned.

'He must have had many girlfriends while on campus!'

'Halim, his legend goes before him. All the girls were fighting to get to know him. I never saw Halim walking alone—he was aways with an attractive girl!'

'You're not too shabby yourself!' Sofia lifted the satay from the fire.

'We were equal competitors,' Wati conceded.

'Why didn't he marry a girl from the university?' asked Sofia curiously.

'I don't know, Halim was a womaniser—sometimes he would date three girls at once. One night there was a dance on campus. All the girlfriends expected invitations and Halim didn't know what to do. So, he arrived at the party with his first girlfriend and then excused himself, leaving her talking to a friend of his while he collected the second girlfriend. Then he did the same thing with her and collected girlfriend number three. Initially, the three girls did not know Halim had brought all of them all at once. They each thought that Halim was their partner. After they began to talk to each other, the secret came out. Well, you have no idea! The party became chaotic! And the moral of that story is: don't fool around with Halim!'

Sofia nodded slowly but she was thinking about Nora. Could it be that Halim was still the old Halim? Just as Wati, was still the old Wati? This was the question playing in Sofia's head.

'Hey, don't listen to Wati's empty talk!' called Halim. 'I can hear my name being mentioned! Well, this can't be on, gossiping behind my back.'

'If we want to embarrass you, we can talk in front of you,' said Wati.

Halim smiled charmingly and came over.

'Is the satay still hot?' he asked Sofia.

'Hot,' replied Sofia—as hot as her heart and the heat rising in her cheeks.

'Wati hasn't changed, has she, Sofia? I'm not sure about school days, but she's exactly the same as she was at university, only her outfit has changed a little. She used to wear those tight pants. Now she's in a skirt,' said Halim, reaching for the satay.

'And do you know why she was always in those tight pants?' said Salman, coming over.

'Why?' asked Halim, turning to Salman.

31

'It was easier for her to get on someone's motorcycle!' Salman said, laughing.

'You mean your motorcycle!' said Halim.

They laughed. Only Sofia was not laughing. She was bored with this conversation which she found rather offensive. She pretended to tend to the satay.

'Halim is good looking you know,' said Wati turning Sofia who was still silent. 'You need to watch him. He was a Romeo at university!'

'Well, what's there to watch,' said Sofia, 'I'm in the kitchen all day long so how can I watch him when he's is at the office, miles away.'

Wati looked troubled. 'If you were not my best friend, I wouldn't care! But I don't want my own friend to be talked about.'

'What do you mean?' Sofia's curiosity fired up.

'Before, I didn't know that Halim was my best friend's husband, I was only listening to the gossip at the office. But now, when I think about it, it makes me angry.'

'What is it? What did they say?'

'At first, I didn't know, because every time they saw me, they would stop talking. One day I got hold of Ahmad and I asked him seriously.''

'Ahmad?' asked Sofia.

'Ahmad, the office boy in Halim's office. He likes to be informed about the secrets of the officers. Through him I found out a little bit of what they were discussing,' said Wati.

'What did you find out?'

'Ah! One day I will tell you about it. Right now there are too many people, but, what you need to know is that they say you stay at home; you don't know anything. They are attractive and young, you have grown up children. I really didn't want to tell you, but because we have slept on the same bed once I need to advise you. You must take care of your looks. Slim down a little. Pay attention to yourself; you are still attractive and young. Don't be stuck in the kitchen, not knowing what's happening in the city. Don't be a slave in the house, washing dishes, cooking, cleaning the house; the work is never finished. Halim has a big salary so find a maid, let her handle all of it. You look after yourself. Once in a while, come to the office; we can go out to lunch, show yourself to the typists at the office—they think you cannot compete with their looks. At that time you can also show off to Halim.'

'Hey, why the whispers?' called Datin Jamilah. 'Aren't you finished talking yet? I'm jealous.'

'Don't disturb them, datin,' said Halim. 'They want to talk about the past twenty years in two hours.'

Everyone laughed.

'Come on, let's go,' said Datuk Arif, abandoning the card game. 'Even if we sat two more hours we'd not win anything. They are all professionals. We're amateurs, we'll be roughly beaten if we go on.'

'Sofia,' said Datin Jamilah as she got leave. 'Thank you very much, next time if there is satay, do invite us again.'

'You don't need to invite her, the smell of the grilled satay will reach our house. We'll just come over when we smell the satay,' said Datuk Arif as he held out his hand to Sofia.

'Eh, even if there is no satay, do come over—we also have ordinary coffee,' said Sofia.

'Yes, that's right, we're neighbours,' said Datin Jamilah who had just moved near to Sofia's house. 'Do come over to our house Sofia, it's not far.'

'Thank you,' said Sofia.

Halim walked Datuk Arif and Datin Jamilah to their car. The other guests were also shaking hands and leaving.

Rahim turned into Seroja Road. The white BMW could not be seen in the vicinity of Wati's house. The gates were open. Rahim went straight into the yard of house number 849. He turned off the car engine. The takeaway noodles he had brought were still hot. The talk in Kaloi ended rather late and he'd driven straight to Wati's without returning home first. It was a long time since he had seen his wife. A towel and two pairs of clothes were always ready in the back of the car. He could change his clothes anywhere. He could also eat anywhere.

The light outside was on.

'Who is it?' a voice asked.

'Rahim, Wati's husband!' said Rahim.

'Oh, Wati has gone out. Come in,' said the voice from inside

Rahim climbed out of the car with the noodles in his right hand and a bag in his left. The front door opened. Rahim entered.

There was no one there. Rahim sat down heavily in a chair facing the television. He felt really exhausted and he had not taken a bath today. He looked around the house that was neat and clean. Everywhere there were fresh flowers and pots of plants. He wondered who took care of the house in such a careful manner. Wati must have hired an efficient maid.

'Hello!' He heard a voice behind him.

'Hi,' Rahim responded, turning round.

'Sir, you are The Honourable Mr Rahim, aren't you?' said an attractive girl with dimples in her cheeks.

'Yes,' Rahim was still bewildered.

'I am Malisa.'

'Are you staying with Wati?'

'Yes, there are three of us, including Wati,' said Malisa as she sat opposite, 'Wati went out to Mr Halim's house, there's a party there. I thought you would be with her. She left this address with me. She said if you arrive, give this to you, sir.' Malisa handed a piece of paper to Rahim.

'No need to call me 'sir'. Just call me Rahim.'

'Alright Rahim. Wati telephoned from her office earlier. She said she couldn't contact you, but she left a message at the office.'

'Oh, I didn't return to the office. From the talk, I headed here directly.'

Malisa nodded. 'What would you like to drink?'

'Just water, thank you.'

She got up to go to the kitchen.

'Malisa!' Rahim called out.

Malisa turned.

'Can I take a bath?'

'Wati's room is on the right, go right in.'

Rahim got up, reached for his bag and went to the room on the right. He opened the door and smiled: it was very untidy. It had been a while since Rahim had seen such a room. Wati had previously been on a course in Japan. While Wati was there, Rahim was lonely and he got involved more actively in politics till he was selected to be the People's Representative.

This was the second time he'd come to the house. The first time was when he helped Wati to bring her things over.

Rahim did not know where to put his bag. Wati's bed was covered with clothes. He placed the bag by the bathroom door. Malisa was making refreshments in the kitchen and he could hear ice being crushed. His eyes were beginning to feel heavy but he needed to bathe.

Malisa found there was still some of the mung bean porridge she had made earlier. Ah, just serve that. Malisa herself was not feeling hungry. It was already 10.00 o'clock at night. Rokiah her roommate was already asleep.

Malisa waited a while for Rahim to come out looking fresh after the bath.

'Have a drink and some porridge,' Malisa offered.

'Ah you should not have troubled yourself,' said Rahim. 'Oh yes, I bought some noodles earlier. Hmm ... they're probably cold now. I've not had dinner yet.'

'No?' Malisa was puzzled. 'Let me dish some up. If you wait for Wati, you don't know what time she'll be back; it is a party after all.'

'Bring a plate for yourself too. I don't feel like eating alone,' said Rahim.

'Alright, but I've already brushed my teeth.'

Rahim laughed.

Going to the kitchen for plates and cutlery, Malisa could see through the door to Wati's room. The bed was neatly made, her clothes piled nicely. No wonder Rahim took a long time in the shower, he was tidying up after Wati!

Soon Rahim was spooning mung bean porridge into his mouth.

'Eh, isn't that sweet? Eat it after you have had your noodles, want?' said Madam Halimah.

Everyone laughed heartily. Sofia also smiled. It tickled her to see their indignation. But feelings of anger also crept into her heart.

'Of course she wants to get married,' said Madam Shamsiah.

'But of course.' Madam Halimah was not satisfied. 'She wanted the wife to divorce her husband?'

'No,' said Madam Shamsiah. 'That's the thing. She only wanted the wife to allow the husband to marry her.'

'Ooo she wants to become the second wife?' said Madam Ainun.

'If that is so, why the need to ask the wife? The religion does not require permission. It is only us that makes up such a requirement,' said Madam Kalsom.

Datin Zaharah nodded firmly. 'That's right, if we didn't make it so, the men would go overboard. We need to defend our position, too.'

'Perhaps the husband of the woman did not want to marry her, so she herself went to meet the wife of the man,' said Madam Shamsiah.

'At times, men are really daring outside the house, but at home they are cowards,' said Madam Kalsom.

'That's true,' said Madam Halimah, 'but cowards like that are dangerous. With us, they don't dare open their mouths. We may not know a thing even after having two or three children,' said Madam Ainun.

'Yes, do you remember that recent scandal? Only when the husband passed away did the wife know there was another wife. But, what could she do; the husband had slipped the hook, she had no choice but to accept it. She must have been angry, I think,' said Datin Zaharah.

They heard the telephone ring two or three times and Sofia got up to answer it.

'Datin,' she called out, 'someone wants to speak with Madam Shamsiah.'

'Madam, Sham,' said Datin Zaharah, 'there, the second wife is calling!'

'Oh, datin! Don't, datin! Don't say that. I fear your words might come true!' Madam Shamsiah got up and went over to the telephone.

The other wives laughed at the joke.

Sofia sat down again.

'Please have some more refreshments. You're so busy talking about other people that you forgot to eat my savoury cakes.' Datin Zaharah winked. Everyone knew she had not made the savoury cakes; they had been bought from stalls at the roadside. No one had time to make savoury cakes these days.

'So, remember that our main meeting is in April. We're inviting Datin Sabehah, so we must make it a bit grand, not like last year's,' Datin Zaharah said.

Madam Shamsiah hurried over. 'Oh datin!!!!' she said.

'Huh, what's wrong?'

'I forgot to fetch my husband. I promised to pick him up. He wants to use the car! Ohhh....'

'That's what happens when you're too busy talking about other people's husbands. If you're late to pick him up, the secretary might send him,' said Madam Halimah.

'Well, earlier I heard the gentle voice from the office, perhaps that was his secretary?' Sofia interrupted trying to joke.

Sofia did not hear Halim's car. Earlier, she had opened the gates and now she was waiting for Halim to return, reading the newspaper beside the water fountain at the corner of the yard. It was shady and cool there, underneath a tree with thick leaves. Sofia often sat in that spot if she wanted to read magazines or novels in the afternoon.

Halim drove straight into the garage near the kitchen. He saw Sofia at the fountain and thought that surely she was not aware that he had just come home. From the road, Halim had turned off the engine and allowed the car to slide into the parking space. He wanted to surprise Sofia. Halim loved to surprise Sofia. He remembered when he returned from reading the Qur'an once. Halim would hide behind the big tree waiting for her and then shout as loud as he could. Sofia would run after him throwing whatever that was in her hand at him. Halim smiled remembering it.

Halim opened his car door slowly because he did not want Sofia to hear. He walked toward the kitchen placing his briefcase and coat on the table near the stairs. Small cakes and tea had been prepared and layed out on the table. He wondered what kind of pudding Sofia had concocted this time. She loved to cook and tried a different recipe every day.

Engrossed in the newspaper, Sofia heard footsteps and almost screamed because she had just been reading about a housewife who was raped. When she saw that it was only Halim who was walking towards her she leaned back breathing deeply. Halim was carrying the tray with drinks and cakes which she had prepared earlier. He smiled at Sofia's surprise.

'I was wondering who it was!'

Before Sofia could take the tray from Halim, he had already placed it on the table in front of her. 'You're surprised, right?'

'I was just reading about a rape case, that's why I was so jumpy! I didn't even hear you return!' said Sofia. She moved over to allow Halim to sit beside her, 'Do you want to eat here?'

'It's nice eating here! The air is fresh,' said Halim as he poured tea into the cups.

'Not playing golf today?'

'There was a meeting today so they probably couldn't get in touch with me. Besides, once in a while it's nice to sit at home with my wife,' said Halim as he placed his hand on Sofia's thigh.

I really cannot believe it, thought Sofia. I cannot believe that Halim could start an affair with another woman.

'Tell me again, what were you so busy reading that you did not hear me coming in?' asked Halim, peering at the newspaper.

For a moment, caught up in the terror of the story she had just read, Sofia forgot about Nora.

'A house wife was raped!' she said.

'Oh ... rape. Probably the woman was too sexy.'

'Ah! Men are cruel. However evil a man is, the blame is still on the woman,' protested Sofia.

'If the woman is dressed sexily and her body exposed, then she is almost asking for it. If she's afraid of being raped then surely she should dress decently. And besides, who can prove whether it's rape or not? Sometimes the woman takes the initiative. Perhaps the man didn't agree to marry her, so she then claims that the man has raped her. Perhaps she was really the one who wanted it.'

Halim ate some cake and Sofia watched him eat. After what he had just said, she had no appetite; her mind was still on the case.

'Have you heard of that case where a wife accused her husband of raping her?' said Halim.

'A wife accusing a husband of rape!' Sofia was shocked. 'What happened finally?'

'I think the trial's still ongoing. Well, this is in the United States, they take everything to court. The ones who become rich are the lawyers!' Halim helped himself to another cake. 'Ah! I just remembered! Sofia, would you like to come with me to Tokyo?'

Sofia was delighted. It was truly unexpected.

'You're always fooling with me … Ahhh! I don't believe you!'

'Hey, it's genuine! Why would I want to pretend? I have to attend a conference there. The other officials could not go. If you want to come along, you're welcome,' said Halim. He reached for a small leaf that had fallen on Sofia's hair.

Sofia could not believe that Halim wanted to take her to Tokyo with him. Halim had never taken her abroad. This was a wonderful opportunity. If she had not confronted Nora face-to-face, Sofia would not have believed anyone who told her that Halim was having an affair with another woman.

'When are you going?' asked Sofia.

'This April!'

'April?' Sofia was rather disappointed.

'Why?'

'Which date would that be?'

'I'm not sure, what's wrong?'

'Our association is a bit busy this April. We'll be having our annual meeting. Datin Sabehah is coming and all of us must contribute. If I go with you to Tokyo, what would they say? They would surely say something,' said Sofia. The happy face had turned sour.

'Sofia, they wouldn't say anything. It is only a voluntary organisation!'

'You don't understand! I cannot stand it when people talk behind our backs.'

'If you cannot bear it, ignore it. Turn a deaf ear.'

'We may not want to hear things, but they still reach us.'

'Hmm ... I really don't understand women. Always gossiping about others!'

Sofia shook her head. 'Hey, don't say that! Men are far worse when it comes to criticising others!'

Now it was Halim's turn to protest. 'Where did you get that idea? We're not like that at all!'

'It's not as if I don't know! If you speak to Ramli, everyone will be mentioned,' said Sofia.

They could hear a car honking. Halim and Sofia turned to look at the gates, which were opened wide.

'It's Wati!' said Sofia, rising immediately.

Wati turned off the car engine at the roadside.

'Hello! Wow ... like *Romeo* and *Juliet* here!' called Wati, walking toward the gates with a file under her arm.

Sofia walked out to greet her. 'Come in. Why did you park the car outside?'

'It's alright, Malisa and Rokiah are in the car. We're all going to Kaloi. They want to see Kaloi Village,' said Wati. She was wearing blue trousers with the legs rolled up to the knees.

'You want to go to the village dressed in trousers like that?' asked Sofia.

'Well, I'll only be in the car. When we arrive, it will be night time. The villagers will not see me,' said Wati.

'Come in for a while! Invite your friends to come in!' urged Sofia.

'We're in a hurry, I don't want to arrive too late at night. Can you give this file to Halim? Tell him when he has finished reading it, sign it at the bottom,' said Wati, handing over the file to Sofia.

'Don't you want to give it to him? He's just reading the newspaper over there.' Sofia turned towards her husband. 'Halim!'

'Ah! No need ... if there's any problem, ask him to call me in Kaloi!' said Wati.

'Alright ... Drive carefully! Don't drive too fast!'

Wati smiled as she opened her car door. 'When are you coming to Kaloi?'

'One day,' said Sofia as she closed Wati's car door.

Sofia watched the BMW turn into the main road. Wati, is lucky to have a husband who is as patient as Rahim. Wati goes here and there, and they only meet once in a while, but Rahim is faithful to her.

Sofia remembered her acrimonious meeting with Nora again. She wanted to ask Halim about it but Halim had never previously hurt her, so why should she create trouble? Halim was mostly a loving husband. It would be better for Sofia to just forget about the Nora episode. What good was there for her to think about something that she coulldn't change. Why should she seek trouble?

5

WATI drove in the direction of Sofia's house. She was really busy that day. The telephone had been ringing continuously. There was a meeting at the Putra Building. When her mind was on work, Wati could not do anything else. Now she thought about Hisham, her only child who was schooling in Kuala Kangsar. Guilt crept into her heart. Hisham was staying in a boarding school. He would surely not feel lonely but still she knew she had often ignored him. Hisham had grown up without her care. When he was small, he had to live with his grandmother in the village because they did not have a helper to take care of him. Later, Hisham had really wanted to stay in a boarding school. Wati had to let him for the sake of his own future but sometimes now she found herself wondering whether she had lost something important.

Wati turned her white BMW into Sofia's yard. Sofia was already outside the house looking at her orchids. When she saw the BMW drive in, she turned and walked towards the car.

Wati did not turn the engine off. From a distance, Sofia could see that Wati was wearing a corn coloured scarf and red lipstick. She had her hair tied to one side and coiffed. Sofia opened the car door and observed the tight blue jeans Wati had bought from Tokyo. Her high heeled shoes were also the colour of corn.

'Wow, Wati, you look like a movie star,' said Sofia, as

she sat down.

'Sofia, we are still young, don't think that we are old. We're always young.'

'How can you wear your blouse tucked into your tight pants like that? If I wore something like that, there would be a bulge right here,' said Sofia, pointing to her stomach.

'Do *sit ups* twenty times, twice a day.'

'Do *sit ups*?' repeated Sofia, laughing heartily. 'I don't even have time to do *sit downs*!'

'Are you so busy? You shouldn't be like that. You must make time for yourself. If we don't find time for ourselves, who will lose out? We will! However busy I am, I still find time to exercise, go for facials and do my hair. If we don't take care of ourselves, who will? And besides, our husbands want to see their wives neat, clean and attractive.'

'You're absolutely right there, but I don't know... I feel lazy, that's all. Perhaps you take care of your body because you're always outside the house, at the office, in public, as the wife of a dignitary. But I am stuck in the kitchen. Halim seldom takes me out. When he comes home from work, he will sit yawning in front of the TV. Sometimes, he won't even talk to me,' said Sofia.

The car stopped at a junction. The traffic light turned red.

'Sofia, we must not think that a woman's place is only in the home. The world out there is bigger and wider than the kitchen. We cannot depend on our husbands forever. There are wives who do not interact with anyone; they only stay in the house from morning till night. Their world is only their house. Perhaps if they didn't complain, it wouldn't be so bad. But, no. They not only choose to be isolated at home, they also complain that their husbands never want to entertain them. These wives should be more understanding. They should be more understanding about their husbands' work and responsibility. Of how tiring a day's work in the office can be. The wives must know how to make themselves happy,' said Wati.

'Hmm, that's a really long speech from the lecturer this time,' said Sofia smiling.

'Forgive me, Sofia. Sometimes we need to analyse why we behave this way or that way. We need to go to the source. If we do, it's easy for us to solve the problem.'

'The problem is, madam doctor, I am tired with life. Life is just empty, meaningless. In short, madam doctor, I am bored stiff.'

The car was already in the middle of the big city but Sofia hadn't yet noticed, too caught up in the conversation.

'You say that you're bored with life. You must identify the causes. If you know the causes, it will be easier for you to deal with them,' said Wati as she turned the car to the right.

Sofia knew the real cause but she did not want to discuss her husband's affair with another woman. Sofia had her dignity. If she talked about the affair, that would mean she had admitted defeat, that she was no longer able to defend her castle from the threats of enemies. Halim was her castle and Nora was the enemy that was attacking every minute. She wouldn't admit defeat but she also sensed that she was not strong enough to stop the attacks. Was she so unattractive? Did she really not know how to attract her own husband? Sofia believed that everything within her was enough to defend her castle.

Now she shook herself and tried to change the topic.

'Oh, I've not asked you where we're heading?' said Sofia,

looking forward.

'We're already here,' said Wati.

They turned into the yard of a big tall building and found a parking space.

'Where is this?' asked Sofia.

'Do you want something to drink first?' asked Wati, ignoring Sofia's question.

'I already had tea before you arrived.'

'If that's the case, here is what we'll do. I want to have my hair washed first. If you want to wash your hair, you may too; you may also have a facial or a body massage. They have everything here.'

'A beauty spa? O.K. I'll accompany you first, after that I'll think about what I'd like to do... Hmm, the body massage, how's that?'

'Eh if you've not tried it, you'd not know. They have a body grooming place too,' said Wati.

Sofia followed Wati up the stairs. Her confused thoughts were becoming clearer. She was relieved and happy to be with an old friend who was honest and sincere. Nowadays it was difficult to find a true friend. Sofia felt lucky to have met Wati again after being separated for such a long time.

There was a knock on the door.

'Come in,' Halim's eyes were still on the paper on the table.

'How busy you look!' said Nora, coming in and closing the door to Halim's room.

'Eh, why do you close the door? Someone might want to

come in,' said Halim, still busy writing.

'Who wants to come in? Everyone has gone home. Isn't it five o'clock already? I waited for you downstairs, Ahmad said you were still busy writing. What are you so busy about?'

'I don't know...everything... the work is endless. Sometimes I think I must work twenty-four hours,' said Halim. 'There's not even time to go home!'

Nora sat down. 'That's what happens when you insist on an isolated house far from the city, so you can live among the wealthy.'

Halim paid no attention to Nora's words. He was used to her jokes, the way she teased him with her bright eyed smile.

'I once asked Ramli to find me a flat near the office so that I could go there if I had to work late at night.'

Hearing Halim's words, Nora's heart skipped a beat. This was her chance to trap Halim. She was getting wilder now.

Men could not be trusted, thought Nora. If he changes his mind, I will lose my chance. *Ala*, Sofia ... what's there with Sofia? Would Sofia allow Halim to take another wife? I cannot miss this chance.

'There's a vacant flat near here. It was only recently vacated,' said Nora, playing with the pen on Halim's desk.

'Really?'

'If you're serious, I can enquire for you.'

'Hey, I am serious. Absolutely. Please handle it. If you think the place is suitable then that's fine, I don't need to see it,' said Halim.

He continued writing, paying her no more attention. Nora prepared hot coffee which was Halim's favourite. She brought it to the table. 'Hmm, still not finished! Isn't your back sore?'

'Quite sore. The nerve on my neck feels really tense.'

Nora moved behind him and began to massage Halim's shoulders with both her hands. Halim stopped writing and closed his eyes. The tensed nerves were beginning to relax.

'Hmmmm ... that feels really good. Hmm ... if someone will massage me like this all night, I can finish my work,' said Halim.

'Ah, who would want to be with you all night?'

'Eh, where are you going?'

'*Ala*, nowhere. Where would I go if not with you?' said Nora. She had simply wanted to test Halim's affections.

Halim looked up and smiled at Nora's pretty face as she stood there behind him.

'Thank you, Nora,' said Halim. He reached up to take hold of the hands that were still on his shoulders.

'Would you like to come with me to Tokyo?' Halim asked Nora. 'I have a conference there for a week. This time noone else from our company is coming. But if you want to come, no one must know,' said Halim.

'Really!' Nora was elated beyond words. 'Are you serious?'

'Of course. I'm not joking. If you want to come along, apply for leave.'

'On which date?'

'I'll look at my diary and let you know. Prepare warm clothing. It's cold over there you know.'

'Isn't cold good for my complexion?' said Nora, massaging Halim's shoulders more forcefully so that he smiled.

'Hey, I'm hungry. Do you think the canteen's already closed?'

'It's closed,' said Nora.

'There are no biscuits either...'

'Do you want to go out and eat?'

63

'My work isn't done. I won't not be happy until it's completed. I don't want to go anywhere.'

'Why don't I run out and buy you something? There are lots of places near the flat I was telling you about.'

Halim nodded. 'And Nora? Please ask about the rent too. You may tell them I would like to rent starting next month.'

'O.K.,' said Nora, 'I'll go now.'

Closing Halim's door, Nora felt truly happy, as though she owned the world. Her soul felt as if it might floating away with happiness. Tokyo! Tokyo! Nora had never been overseas, had never been anywhere. She felt her dreams would come true. Furthermore, Halim wanted to rent the flat. Nora could go there often. Indeed, she must visit it frequently before another woman was brought there. Now only Nora knew about the matter. The place was a secret. Wati would not know! ... Sofia would not know!

'Wow! Sofia! You look so gorgeous.... That hairstyle really suits you. No one would think that you've got a grown up child,' said Wati.

Sofia smiled.

'Did you have a facial?'

'Yes!'

'Eh, look at that! Who would have thought you were this pretty. That's what I have been saying, don't let only the kitchen smoke get you!'

'Ala, even if I'm pretty, who would look at me?' said Sofia as she got up to check her complexion in the large mirror.

'Invite your husband to have dinner with you at a restaurant, or big hotel,' said Wati.

'My husband's working late tonight. 'Probably' he won't come home to eat. And if he said 'probably' that means 'definitely' not coming home for dinner,' said Sofia, as she reached for her handbag.

'Okay, then let's go to the Universe Hotel. The food is good there, the music wonderful,' said Wati, getting up.

'Eh, with these clothes on?'

'Look, if you're pretty and your smile attractive, you can wear anything. People look at our smiles, they forget to look at other things. Come on, let's go!'

The grey Mercedes turned towards house number 849, Seroja Road. Rahim knew Wati had not arrived home yet because her BMW was not in the parking area. There was a dinner in Kaloi; the Chief Minister would also be attending. It wouldn't be appropriate to arrive without Wati. He had called several times at the office but without success. She always seemed to be in a meeting.

'Eh, aren't you coming in!' He heard a voice from the door.

Rahim realised that he had not got out of the car. Perhaps Wati would be a little late. I'll go in first, wait for her for a while, thought Rahim. He got out and stretched, calling out 'Hello'.

Malisa, standing in the doorway, responded to the greeting with a smile. She watched Rahim take his briefcase from the car. He held out a bunch of rambutan and a packet of palm sugar which he had brought from Kaloi. Malisa accepted it gratefully.

'Who is that?' Rokiah's voice was heard from inside.

'Rahim!' answered Malisa.

'Wati's not in,' said Rokiah, as she appeared in the middle of the house.

'What time did she leave?' asked Rahim.

'I guess around 3.00 in the afternoon,' said Rokiah. 'Please sit down.'

'Rahim, what would you like to drink?' Malisa asked, 'Tea or coffee?'

'Black tea will do, thank you. I'm only troubling you,' said Rahim sitting down. 'Wati cannot keep still, that's why she wants to stay together with Miss Rokiah and Miss Malisa. If she lived alone, people would know that the house was always empty.'

Rokiah smiled. 'You drove directly from Kaloi?'

'Yes, there's a big dinner there tonight. Wati needs to attend because the Chief Minister will be there.'

'That sounds rather difficult. Wati said she was going to town to have her hair set. Perhaps she's getting ready to go to Kaloi!'

'I'm not sure, I'm afraid she might have forgotten. My secretary tried to call her at the office this morning but she was out at a meeting... ' Rahim sounded rather anxious. He tapped his fingers against his leg. 'I haven't had time to pray. I'll do that first. Excuse me.'

Rahim stood up and went directly to Wati's room. It was in the same state as usual: cosmetics strewn all over the place, clothes everywhere. Rahim went directly to the bathroom. He was trying to think straight. What should he do if Wati returned home late? The Chief Minister's wife had told him earlier that she'd like to meet Fatimawati. What excuse could he give her this time?

'You managed to cook the sago?' asked Rokiah. 'Where did you get the palm sugar?'

'Rahim brought it with him and I thought I might as well use it. If we had to wait for Wati, the palm sugar would go bad. I think she's afraid to ever come into the kitchen!' said Malisa.

'That's true,' said Rokiah.

Malisa brought out black tea and the sago. She found Rahim waiting in the living room. 'This is the palm sugar you brought today.'

'The palm sugar I brought? You made that very quickly, Malisa, how did you do it?'

Malisa smiled. 'I just blink twice, and the food is ready, of course. Isn't that what you men think?'

'Why did you bring only one cup of tea? How about Miss Rokiah and you? Are you not having tea with me?'

'We're trying to slim down,' said Rokiah.

'If so, I don't want any either. It's embarrassing to come and eat, and drink tea, while the hosts are trying to slim down,' said Rahim.

'Malisa, you have tea with Rahim, I've just had some.'

'I sympathise with you, Rahim, each time you come, Wati is out. It's so far for you to travel; Kaloi is kilometres away,' said Malisa as she spooned some sago into a bowl. Then she poured the palm sugar and oconut milk. Rahim watched, without a word.

Malisa held out the bowl of sago to Rahim.

'Thank you, you should not have troubled yourself, I could do it,' said Rahim as he took the bowl from Malisa's hand.

'It's my pleasure. You must be tired from driving.'

'Aren't you having any, Malisa?'

'Later, I just got home. I arrived shortly before you.'

'Is your office far from here?'

'Not that far, my friend drives me up to the big junction over there.'

Rahim looked at his wristwatch. 'If Wati is not here in the next half hour, I'll have to go without her.'

'You want to go back to Kaloi, Rahim?' asked Malisa.

'Yes, the C.M. is coming to my district. I must be there. How could Wati have forgotten about this? Now, I'm really sure, I gave her plenty of warning. Is she that busy?'

'Well, Wati is really busy!' said Rokiah, appearing in the living room. 'You know, she's an executive! We're only clerks. When office work is done, that's it for us. For the executives, sometimes there are meetings outside, they could be writing reports till late at night. Wati should quit her job. She's already the wife of the People's Representative, she shouldn't be working anymore. She should just stay in Kaloi. There are surely many people who come to the house of the People's Representative. She should receive and entertain them.' said Rokiah, as sat down with them.

Rahim was silent.

'But, Kiah, she's earning a big salary. Why would she want to quit? It's alright with our kind of work. We don't get that much,' said Malisa.

Rahim kept on glancing at his wristwatch. Rokiah and Malisa were unable to do anything. They could only watch anxiously.

'There's no time to search for her. The city is not like Kaloi,' said Rokiah.

'Yes, you're right. In any case I need to get going if I don't want to be late,' said Rahim getting up.

'Alright,' said Rokiah.

Rokiah and Malisa watched Rahim leave. The grey Mercedes drove away. Rahim pressed the accelerator. He was beginning to feel irritated with Wati, who seemed to be treating his wishes and wants lightly. Wati should understand the importance of the C.M.'s visit. Perhaps she did not respect his position as the People's Representative

As he drove, Rahim compared himself with other People's Representatives and began to feel disappointed. His sister was right to say that the wife of the Representative should always try to win the people's heart. But Wati was not even interested in attending a big dinner function in Kaloi.

Yes, Wati is busy! Busy! But today is only a half day, what is making her so busy?

Rahim's heart was heavy as he drove towards Kaloi. The C.M's wife had really wished to meet Wati: what excuse could he give? His body felt drained, his time and energy wasted on a whim. If Wati had informed him earlier that she did not want to attend the dinner, he would not have had to go through all that trouble. Couldn't she have taken two minutes to call him? He was deeply offended but tried to suppress the feelings. He needed to be patient and calm. He needed appear cheerful before the C.M. and his wife. Rahim could not be thinking of Wati. If he thought about his wife, the feeling of disappointment would flare up again.

Wati turned the car into Selasih Road feeling truly satisfied that she had been able to please her friend. She wondered what it was that caused Sofia to cling to her house. If Wati had not made the effort to get her out, she would surely not have made the first step. If I were forced to stay at home for just one day, I would go mad, thought Wati.

'Halim asked me to go with him to Tokyo in April.' Sofia broke the silence. 'At first I refused to go because Datin Zaharah needed some help with the annual meeting. This time they want to make it special, because Datin Sabehah will be there. But yesterday Madam Sham called saying they were postponing it until May because Datin Sabehah has to plan for her daughter's wedding.'

'Hey, that's wonderful, then you can go to Tokyo. In fact, I'd already booked plane tickets for both of you, so now there's no need for me to cancel the booking.' Wati turned the BMW in front of Sofia's gates and switched off the engine.

'But I've already told Halim I won't be going,' said Sofia.

'Ah, never mind! He never asked me to cancel the ticket? There's no problem. If you don't have time to buy a winter overcoat, use mine!'

Sofia was still quiet.

'You don't have to think about it. How often do we get the chance to go on a second honeymoon? If I were you, I wouldn't let it slip away,' said Wati.

'Alright,' said Sofia as she opened the car door, 'are you coming in?'

'No thanks.' Wati started the car. 'Good night and see

you soon!'

'Good night, thank you,' said Sofia.

The white BMW drove away and Sofia stepped into the house. She didn't know that Halim had only just arrived home.

'Have you had dinner?' Sofia asked Halim, who was reading a newspaper in the living room.

'Yes,' said Halim without looking up.

'Have you finished your proposal?'

'Yes.'

'I went out with Wati, we had dinner at the Universe Hotel.'

Only then did Halim look up and see Sofia's new hairstyle, her glowing skin.

'Hey, who's this movie star?'

'Oh, please don't tease me!' said Sofia.

'I can see you've been hanging out with Wati, you've become modern like her,' said Halim as he put down the newspaper.

'So, previously I was old-fashioned?'

'No, who said you were old-fashioned?'

'When are you leaving for Tokyo?' asked Sofia. She wanted to tell him that she had changed her mind and decided to come and she waited for Halim to encourage her. But Halim neither encouraged nor even asked her.

'Maybe the twelfth,' said Halim. He opened the newspaper again. He was afraid to talk about Tokyo now.

Sofia was silent. She understood the opened newspaper as an indication that this conversation between them had ended. Halim did not have time to discuss his conference in Tokyo.

Sofia was disappointed; she felt as though Halim was

ignoring her. So she left him. She knew when Halim wanted to be alone. She went to her room and stood facing the closet mirror. As she studied from different angles her face with the new hairdo, a feeling of regret emerged in her heart. Halim didn't look twice at me even though I am this attractive. He found the newspaper more important. He was too tired to answer my questions. He didn't want to talk long. Why don't I want to accept the truth? Why don't I accept the fact that I am old?

Halim naturally wants a woman who is more attractive, younger like Nora. What would he want with me who's already old? Sofia's heart felt sadder, disappointed beyond words.

She went downstairs again past Halim still reading his newspaper. Halim did not even see Sofia go outside. She went to the bench beneath the mango tree near the bamboo clusters. There she sat down and looked at the full moon bright in the sky. She remembered being in this place with Halim, holding hands, making promises that they would love each other and be together forever. Now, where had all that undying love gone to? Where worth the promises and vows?

Sofia made a decision. She would not seek the fulfilment of those promises. If Halim's heart had changed, Sofia would not put pressure onhim. Love should be felt spontaneously and not demanded or forced.

But I must be firm about the promise that I make to myself, she thought. I promise to nurture my love for Halim so that it will thrive. So that it will not wilt in the sun. I promise to go through all the gales, storms and waves so that true love will be there always throughout my life. But with one condition: that Halim still loves me.

The Wife

The moment I sense any change in Halim, the moment I know that Halim no longer loves me, I will let him go from my heart. At that moment my love and being will be buried.

From a distance she could hear the lovely music from the neighbour's organ. It reminded her of the time when she was young, unmarried, still living in a school hostel and giggling in the dark with Wati. Sofia got up and moved into the house.

Halim was sleeping on the sofa. His newspaper had fallen to the floor. Sofia went over to him. She remembered when they were newlyweds and would always be near each other like this, sitting together as they read books and magazines.

'Poor Halim', whispered Sofia. Gently she touched her husband's forehead. She massaged it lovingly.

Halim opened his eyes slowly. Sofia's pretty face looked blurred.

'Sofia!' said Halim. He held Sofia's hand. ''What's wrong?' he asked.

'Come and sleep upstairs. It's uncomfortable here,' said Sofia. She was offended again. When they were younger, Halim would never ask if there was anything wrong. Sofia touched him lovingly. Yes, it is true I am approaching old age. I am not as pretty as before, I am not beautiful. Halim got and climbed the stairs. He did not turn toward Sofia who was still sitting on the sofa.

Yes, I am indeed getting old!

6

'**WELL**, Halim! So how long have you been close with that girl Nora?' asked Ramli.

'Hey what are you suggesting, doesn't she work in this building? Sometimes she has to communicate with me on matters regarding the office,' said Halim.

'Halim, please don't think that everyone's blind. I can see that she's after you,' said Ramli.

'She's knows that I'm married with a kid. I have reminded her about my position. What is there for me to fear?'

'Who said you were afraid? It's not your bravery that I question'

'I've done anything wrong.'

'Yet!' Ramli gave a meaningful smile.

'Ramli, even you don't trust me?'

'I know you very well. I've known you for a long time,' said Ramli.

'But, that was then. This is now.'

'What's the difference between then and now?'

'Well, then I was young, even handsome.'

'I ask again, what's the difference? In fact, it's better than before. You have a high position, a big car. In the old days, girls would even get on your scooter, so why would they hesitate when you've got a big car. Then there was no money, now there's plenty of money.'

'If I think about my younger days...' Halim laughed heartily. 'I remember one night when my scooter ran out of gas in the middle of the road and I didn't have any money. Thank God I had already seen my date home!'

'Who?' asked Ramli.

'I don't know ... can't remember her name, but it was the first date.'

'Huh ... and after that?'

'After she had cleaned me out?'

'That night you had to treat her, I suppose?'

'Eh, the first date, of course I would pay. But I didn't expect my pockets to be emptied.'

'Hmm that's what was wrong with you, you had no money but you acted like a rich man!'

'Others were doing it, I just wanted to join in,' said Halim.

'Then, what happened?'

'Fortunately, I found a few coins. And luckily, Razillah had a car...'

'Razillah? Who was that'

'The girl who used to pick me up at college in her car!'

'Oh yes, I remember her; the daughter of a rich man!'

'I had to walk a bit to the telephone booth. Fortunately she was home. I asked her to come and get me,' said Halim.

'She came to pick you up in the middle of the night? Wasn't her mother angry with her?'

'Don't you remember her parents were in London. Her father worked there!'

'Oh, then, she was free?'

'Hmm, she lived with her housemaid and younger siblings. She could do what she wanted,' said Halim.

'So it was Razillah who you were really close to?'

'I don't make the mistake of being too close with women Ramli. If you're tied down, you'll regret it.'

'Oh so that's why you are totally free!'

'That was then,' said Halim, trying to hide the truth.

'Well, well, well!' From far, they could a voice interrupting Ramli's and Halim's conversation.

'Oh Wati, *datin*!' said Halim.

Ramli and Halim got up to pull a chair for Wati and Datin Sarina.

'Isn't *datuk* here today?' asked Ramli.

'He's here with *Tan Sri*, still hitting over there. We're playing with a group of women today,' said Datin Sarina taking out a handkerchief from her handbag.

Halim turned to Wati who was still silent. 'Anything to drink?'

'Hmm, yes, I'd like iced tea,' said Datin Sarina.

'Lychee!' said Wati.

Halim hailed the waiter and ordered the refreshments.

'Halim, why didn't you bring your wife to play golf with us? You're always keeping her locked up at home. Bring her along ... healthy mind, healthy body,' said Datin Sarina.

Wati turned toward Halim, but remained silent.

'*Datin*, it's difficult to bring women to play golf!' said Halim.

'Wati, look at him. He dares to say that to us!'

'If all the women were here playing golf, it would be really crowded, datin, we men would not have the chance to play,' said Halim.

'You and your excuses, Halim!' Datin Sarina knew he liked to joke.

'Never mind, we'll build another golf course for women,'

said Ramli, trying to offer a solution.

'That's right *datin*, think about it, if everyone here today brought their wives, wouldn't it be crowded?' said Halim.

'Men play golf because they want freedom, to escape from the home. If they're at home, their wives are always asking them to do things. On the golf course, it's peaceful, isn't it? If you're upset with the boss, hit the ball harder. Release that anger,' said Wati.

'It can't be that bad!' said Ramli.

'Men like to assert their identity as men,' said Halim, beginning to be serious.

'Isn't it asserted now?' asked Datin Sarina, with a meaningful smile.

Everyone laughed.

'Did I say anything wrong? For so long now women have wanted to compete with men. In almost all fields that men have explored, women also want to test themselves. Soon, men will no longer know which field is to be considered manly, something to be proud of,' said Halim.

'Yes, that's also true, if women want to enter all fields, men will be forced to stay home and cook,' said Ramli.

'I never thought that you were with the anti-women movement,' said Datin Sarina.

'What's the need for Malaysian women to follow their western counterparts? Their culture is different from our culture. Men in Malaysia are different from those in the west; likewise the women. Our thoughts are different, our ways is different, our lifestyle is different. What do our women want to be free from?' asked Halim.

'Yes, that's right, I've never asked that: what do women want to be free from. What's trapping them?' Datin Sarina began to think.

Wati remained silent.

'Just take a look at Wati! She's got all the freedom she needs. Look at yourself, *datin*, you're free to do anything and datuk supports it,' said Halim.

'Hmm, I never thought of that,' said Datin Sarina.

'But what about your wife, Halim?' asked Wati.

'Sofia is free to go anywhere. I give her total freedom. If she wanted to play golf, I would not stop her, but she doesn't want to,' said Halim.

'Why are those awful western women demanding freedom?' asked Ramli.

'You know well that the people there do not interact as we do. Look at us now, we're interacting like this, each of us can say what we want to say, to calm ourselves down,' said Wati. 'Western people do not like to interact like we eastern people. They lose the intimacy that's so significant for the soul.'

'Yes,' said Halim. 'In the West, there was someone who sued her own mother in court.'

'Hmm, if they can bring their own mother to court, what's left in life for her?' asked Datin Sarina.

Wati nodded. 'If we cannot respect our own mothers in this life then who else is left?'

'That may be the difference between the eastern and western countries,' said Ramli. 'Here, we respect our elders, we value feelings of love. Perhaps, that's why our women don't feel they've lost their freedom; they don't feel the pressure because they're admired and respected.'

'Yes, maybe that's the reason. Women in Malaysia hear that Western women have associations, movements for women's rights etcetera, so they also get busy discussing them,' said Datin Sarina. 'But they don't understand the problems that gave rise to such forms of protest. Matters such as those are not found in our country, that's why we don't know what we should protest about.'

'That's why, *datin*, we should no longer look to the West. We should rid ourselves of outdated opinions: you know, thinking that whatever comes from the west is excellent,' said Wati.

'Ah, here comes *datuk*!' Halim got up to get a chair.

'No need Halim!' said Datuk Kassim. 'We've got dinner tonight! Did you forget, Sarina?'

'Yes, that's right! Puan Sri Kamsiah's house!' said Datin Sarina.

They all got up.

'O.K. See you soon!' Datin Sarina waved her hand as the Mercedes sports drove away from the parking lot of the golf club.

'Hmm ... how about you? Who did you come with?' Halim asked Wati.

'I picked datin up from her house. Why, do you want a ride? I would also like to see Sofia for a while. She asked me to buy her something. You know I'm always busy, there's no time to shop.'

'If that's so, Ramli, I'm going back with Wati. You don't have to drop me off,' Halim told Ramli.

'Alright, if that's the case,' said Ramli. 'I'll make a move now.'

'O.K.,' said Wati.

'Thank you,' said Halim. 'Don't forget, how many balls you owe me!'

'Hmm ... I did lose badly today,' said Ramli as he walked away.

Sofia was wiping her hand with the towel hanging near the kitchen door when she heard the telephone ring. Quickly, she rushed over to it. Perhaps, Rahmah was calling. She picked up the telephone.'Hello!'

'Is Halim there?' She could hear a gentle voice.

'Is that Nora?' asked Sofia, bravely. Her heart was beating fast.

'Oh, Sofia!' Nora began.

'Who else would answer? If you call my house, of course it would be me!' said Sofia angrily.

'It's alright if Halim is not in,' said the voice from the other side.

'If it's not you Nora, then it must be Zaitun,' said Sofia. She knew it was Nora on the line but wanted to make her jealous. There was no Zaitun.

'Zaitun!' She could hear the confusion in Nora's voice.

'Is that Zaitun?' Sofia pretended not to know Nora's voice 'I'm sorry, I thought it was Nora. Well, just an office girl who keeps disturbing Halim, but you know him well, Halim is like that. Why are you calling? Halim's not there yet? He said he was dropping by your house earlier.'

'It's not Zaitun!' said Nora. Sofia smiled.

'If not Zaitun, then it's probably Dahlia. Well, it's hard to keep up, Halim has too many women friends!' said Sofia. She knew Nora was angry, but she did not care because she was the one who was supposed to be angry, not Nora.

'Sofia, this is Nora; Nora who you met once,' said Nora, firmly.

'Oh, Nora. Next time, you call, please be direct. Then there won't be any confusion. Well, Halim is also to blame. I don't understand why he needs so many women friends. I'm amazed.' Sofia was aware that she was lying, but she was too angry with Nora's attitude for daring to call Halim at home.

'Let me say something, Sofia; my car stalled by the roadside. I thought, if Halim's around, maybe he can help me...'

'And if he was around, he would surely go and help you. But now he's not here. Miss Nora, if I were a pretty girl like you, I would not call someone's husband for help. Anyone would be happy to help a woman as beautiful as you who's stuck on the road.' Sofia hung up, though she knew Nora had not finished talking.

The nerve! Asking Halim to come and help her because her car had broken down by the roadside. If Halim was around he'd dash right off to help, thought Sofia. And if I knew it was Nora calling, I would follow to see a little of what's going on. But if Halim was the one who answered the telephone, he would not tell me where he would be going. Yes, I would surely never know.

She heard a car honking outside the gates. Perhaps it was Wati. Sofia went to the door in time to see Halim opening the gates and Wati driving her car inside.

'How fantastic you are, like a big boss!' Sofia greeted Halim. 'One driver came to pick you up, and another driver drove you home....'

'Well you know how it is!' said Halim, lost for words. He

opened the car door for Wati.

'Well, were you playing golf?' asked Sofia approaching Wati who was getting out of the car. Halim closed the door behind her.

'Hmm, what else? Earlier, *datin* telephoned to ask me to pick her up. What could I do?' said Wati.

'Well, if the boss' wife has invited you, what can you say?' said Sofia.

'Her wish is my command.'

'Come in,' said Halim going straight through to the kitchen.

Sofia and Wati were still at the door. Halim knew before they entered the house there would be a long talk. He was used to helping his wife with the refreshments.

After meeting Wati, Sofia momentarily forgot Nora and her phone call.

Halim appeared with a tray of cold rose syrup drinks.

'Well, how industrious your beloved Mr Halim is. Hmm, what more do you want?'

Sofia who was standing with her back to Halim turned. She smiled seeing Halim placing the tray on the table.

'I saw that you two were busy discussing clothes and make-up items so I thought I'd get on with things,' said Halim.

'Well, if the rose syrup was prepared by our Mr Halim, I must try it,' said Wati, followed by Sofia.

'There are also some curry puffs!' said Halim. 'Please have some.'

They sat at the table. Wati ate a curry puff.

'Hmm it's really good. Mr Halim is really good at making curry puffs,' Wati said, glancing at Sofia who was smiling.

The Wife

'Well, what am I not good at; I can do anything,' said Halim grinning.

Sofia looked away. She was thinking about Nora again, about her husband's relationship with that petite woman.

'Oh yes, Sofia, Datin Sarina asked you to play golf with her. She said all you ever do is sit at home,' said Wati as she sipped the sweet drink.

'Wati, I am busy with my association. There are always meetings, how can I play golf? I need to take care of the house. It's alright with datin, she has maids, so she can do anything!' said Sofia.

'You yourself don't want a maid,' reminded Halim.

'Yes, I know, having a maid is difficult, not having one is also difficult.' Sofia didn't want a maid because she worried that the maid would not understand Halim's 'friendly' nature. No way, dangerous ... dangerous, thought Sofia.

'Yes, it was difficult for me to get a maid too a long time ago, that's why Hisham had to be cared for by his grandmother!' said Wati.

Halim stared at her. 'You know, Wati, whenever you mention Hisham I get a shock. It's only then I'm reminded that you're a married woman.'

'Well, even if you're married, if you didn't take care of your own children, it could feel like you have no children,' said Sofia.

'It's not just that, she doesn't have her husband either,' said Halim.

'I don't know, Halim. People work; so I wanted to work, people marry; I also wanted to marry, people have children; I also wanted to have children. But everyone's situation is different,' said Wati.

'Well, that's life,' said Sofia.

'Sometimes I feel envious seeing my other friends and their lives. They've got everything. A good husband, smart children, they also have permanent jobs; but what about me? Theoretically, I have everything, but the reality is, there's nothing,' said Wati.

'That's the oddity of life,' said Sofia. She then thought about her own life chasing after shadows. Sofia wanted a husband who was loyal, but what about Nora? Nora was proof that her husband was not loyal.

'Don't think of all that,' said Halim. 'Human beings can't have everything. If a human being had everything he wanted, all ambitions achieved, he'd be so bored with his life that it would become meaningless for him. His spirit would die even though he'd still be moving on this earth.'

Wati appeared not to be listening to Halim. She was lost in her own thoughts. She did not want to die spiritually. She did not want to move with an empty soul without hopes and goals, without wants and desires, without direction.

Rahim, even though he's far away ... wherever I am, he's in my heart. Even when I'm with my friends, my thoughts would always be with him.

'Halim ... can I use your telephone?' asked Wati.

'Yes, go ahead,' said Halim.

Wati went over to the telephone. Halim looked towards Sofia. Sofia pretended to look elsewhere. She was still affected by the telephone call from Nora.

Halim got up, walked toward the stairs and went directly to his room. Sofia held the newspaper which she had not finished reading.

'Hello, Rahim!'

'Hi ... Wati! My goodness. Well this is totally unexpected!'

'Eh which girl did you think it was?' asked Wati.

'What are you talking about?'

'When are you coming?'.

'What's wrong, darling?'

'Nothing.' Wati suddenly felt a pang of sorrow. She felt lonely.

'Wati, do you want me to come back?' asked Rahim.

'Won't you be tired driving?' asked Wati looking at her watch. 'Why not come back early morning tomorrow.'

'Never mind. I'll come back now.'

'O.K., I'll be waiting at home.' Wati put the telephone down and went over to Sofia, who was reading the newspaper.

'I have to go now,' she said, reaching for her hand bag.

'Have some dinner first,' said Sofia.

'No thanks, I've got something on later.'

'Well, don't leave it too late, Wati, take care!'

Wati deliberately did not tell Sofia that Rahim was on his way back. Wati walked toward the door. Sofia followed her to the car.

'When are you coming over again?' asked Sofia.

'We'll see, I can't really make any promises at the moment. Whenever I can come, I'll just come,' said Wati.

'Alright,' said Sofia. 'See you soon.'

The white BMW drove away. Sofia watched Wati leaving. She knew that Wati was also going through some challenges in life but at least her husband was faithful. As for Halim...

She stopped. It was frightening to think about Halim.

Halim treats me no different, always making me happy. He is never rough with me, neither does he raise his voice even when he is angry, she thought. There is no reason for me to be angry with him. But I know for sure that he's having an affair with another girl, someone who is younger and more attractive than me. What should I do? I need to find a solution, I need to find a way to end the anxiety in my heart. But I do not know the way. I do not know how to solve the problem I am facing now.

'Hmm! What's wrong now?' asked Asmah, looking at Nora standing in the door of her room. 'I can see that you're really gloomy. Earlier, when you said you were going out with Halim, you looked cheerful.'

'I called him at home and he wasn't there,' said Nora approaching Asmah who was still in a towel after showering.

'You dared to call him at home?'

'Why would I be afraid?' asked Nora sitting at the edge of Asmah's bed.

'Who picked up the telephone?'

'Who else? Sofia!'

'And then? What did she say?'

'Well, I was really upset with what she said. It got a bit overheated.'

'Hmm, and that was only on the telephone. If you went there, she would put chilli in your mouth, she has the right. If it were my mother, she wouldn't give you a chance!'

said Asmah. She remembered how her mother had struggled to take care of her and her younger siblings because of an irresponsible father.

'Ah, you and your stories about your mother. This is Sofia, not your mother.'

'Why are you so angry with Halim's wife? She should be angry with you, not you with her. You've got this topsy-turvy. I really don't understand. What did she say that upset you so?' asked Asmah as she put cold powder on her face.

'Can you believe, Asmah, she mentioned the names of all these women who're supposedly always calling Halim? I don't believe Halim has affairs with anyone else other than me, I just don't believe it.'

'Hey, why are you so jealous now? If his own wife is not jealous, why should you be?'

'Isn't it obvious? Jealousy means love. I'm jealous because I love Halim. His wife is not jealous, because she has no love for him. Because of this lack of love, Halim is with me. I can give him the love he needs.'

'Hmm ... what else do you give?'

'You're rambling!' said Nora, beginning to be angry.

'You need to remember Nora, he's someone's husband. If you try to seduce him, you'll be committing a sin because you're trying to break up a marriage.'

'Tell me this, why should there be marriage when there's no love? There's no marriage without love.'

'How do you know his wife doesn't love him?'

'When a man seeks another woman, that's a sign that he's not getting love from his wife,' said Nora attending to her long fingernails.

'Hmm! You're so immature, Nora, you still don't

understand what men are like. The truth is that men can never be happy with only one woman. Love, or not, that's not the question. Men are simply like that!'

'Ah, you're the immatureone. You don't even have a boyfriend, do you?' asked Nora.

'Because I've had enough of men, I'm bored with them. I'd rather not have a husband, if it only causes me pain,' said Asmah.

'Then you'll remain single till you die.'

'Ah, life is not as narrow as you perceive. Human beings don't live just to get married; there are other reasons to keep living. Anyway, for me that's not what I want in life. I'm happy with my work at the hospital. I see my patients as my own children. I'm happy I can contribute this way, I feel that my life is filled with meaning.'

'Now, perhaps, you feel that way,: said Nora, 'but what about when you're retired later on with no husband, no children, no grandchildren? Your home will be empty. When you're old, who will care for you when you become ill?'

'I may not live that long. If I do then I will simply live out my days in an old folks' home. Don't forget, I'll still be receiving money every month and when you have money, people will take care of you.'

Asmah stood up. Nora realised that her friend didn't want to talk about the future. Asmah had had enough of men who behaved like her father. She heard the door closing; Asmah had left the room. Perhaps she had gone to the kitchen to get a drink.

She thought about what Sofia had said: Sofia! Sofia, a cruel woman! Her words were hurtful, horrid! She was an insolent woman. Ah, what do I care about her. If I were Halim's wife, I would not allow Halim to have an affair with another woman. I would watch him carefully, I would love him fully. Halim likes to be caressed, to be loved. Sofia definitely won't do that! Sofia is as hard as stone. She is fierce. No man likes a woman who has a heart of stone. I know Halim has been deprived of love. He needs a wife like me, a truly loving wife and a wife who loves him with all her heart.

Wati was waiting for Rahim. She was wearing a long dress which she had just bought from a boutique near the Universe Hotel. She thought about her conversation with Halim that afternoon. Yes, this time Wati felt really lonely. When she was at Halim's house she'd voiced the secrets of her heart which had long been suppressed. She was envious of her happily married friends. Even though she was married, her life was like someone who was not married.

The love that had long ago set root in her heart flared again. She loved Rahim with all her heart. There could not possibly be anything that could come between them.

Wati trusted that Rahim loved her entirely. They had gone through all kinds of trials and tribulations together. Wati thought back to the time when Rahim fell ill while Wati was in the United States. Rahim was lying in hospital, unconscious for several days and Wati knew she had to get home even though it meant ending her PhD studies. She could resume her studies some other time but she would never again find such a husband.

Her tears fell. She heard Rahim's Mercedes enter their

drive. She went outside and locked the door. Malisa and Rokiah had gone for dinner at a nearby roadside stall. Before Rahim could turn off his car engine, Wati was already beside him.

'Hello.' She peered at Rahim, whose hands were still on the steering wheel.

'Hello,' he said.

Wati climbed in and closed the car door.

'Rahim!' Her tears flowed again.

'What's wrong, Wati?' asked Rahim, reaching for his wife's hand.

'I don't know Rahim, I feel upset all of a sudden,' said Wati.

'What happened?' Rahim asked anxiously. The car engine was off. He turned to Wati again. Wati's hands were tightly held.

'I'm lonely without you, without our son, Hisham,' said Wati, crying.

'Yes, I feel the same way. I don't know when we can ever have a normal life like other people.'

'Perhaps it's my fault,' said Wati gazing at Rahim's face in the darkness that was dimly illuminated by the street light.

'No, it's my fault because I doubted your love for me, because I was afraid that you might look down on my previous low position. Because I love you, Wati, I involved myself in politics as this way I could be as good as you.'

Wati stared at Rahim squarely. She recalled how Rahim had fallen ill while she was in the United States continuing her education. Wati understood that Rahim was struggling with himself. He didn't want a position lower than hers. He needed respect from his wife. In the struggle, Rahim had suffered mentally and fallen ill. Wati had returned home and looked after him until he became well.

'Why are you so silent?' said Rahim. 'What're you thinking?'

'I didn't realize until now that your love is so deep that you would go through all that,' said Wati.

She understood now that Rahim had been fighting this battle only to keep her love and respect. If she had known this long ago, she would surely not have gone to the United States and Rahim would surely not have fallen ill; she would surely not have gone to Japan and Rahim would surely not have become a People's Representative; and they would surely not be separated as they were now.

'I will do anything to make you happy, Wati,' said Rahim with certainty.

'I never expected you to come tonight,' said Wati.

'If you wanted, I'd have come even it was from further than Kaloi.'

'Thank you, my love.' Wati placed her head on Rahim's shoulder, looking at the light that was illuminating the road in front of the house. 'You know that you are my one true love?'

'Well, Wati, and do you know how lonely it has been without you by my side? I don't know when we can live together,' said Rahim.

Wati sighed. She felt reassured to be with her husband. She knew that Rahim loved her with all his heart. She squeezed his hand tightly. 'You must be hungry. Let's have something to eat.'

'Alright! Where would you like to have dinner? There's a good steak at the Universe Hotel, there's good fried chicken at the Samudra Hotel.' Rahim started the car.

'At the bank, beside the river, there's delicious *soto* there!' said Wati smiling at Rahim. She touched Rahim's hair which had flopped over his face. Rahim responded with a smile.

'O.K., let's have *soto* at the riverbank. They have a nice iced peanut drink too.'

'You're not embarrassed to eat by the river?' asked Wati. 'I don't know, it might lower your status, the People's Representative having dinner by the river, but driving a Mercedes?'

'As long as I'm with you, Wati, I'll go anywhere.' Rahim turned to look at Wati lovingly.

Wati placed her head on Rahim's shoulder. She held Rahim's arm with both her hands. Oh, Rahim, you are still the same. You are still Rahim whom I loved deeply, you are still Rahim who would do anything for our happiness.

7

SEVERAL times Sofia had tried to inform Halim that she wanted to go to Tokyo but each time she tried to raise the subject, Halim quickly changed it. She couldn't understand why Halim did not want to talk about the conference. Once he had pushed so hard for her to go with him, but now he would not even talk about it.

Sofia knew Wati had not told Halim about Sofia's decision to go to Tokyo. When they discussed it, Wati thought that it would be better if Sofia kept quiet. She said, 'Let Halim get a surprise!' Wati thought that if life was planned at every single moment, it would lose its excitement. But Sofia was was not sure how she felt about surprises. She was not too happy about keeping such a secret from Halim.

Halim was running late and busy putting on his tie. Later that evening, he would be leaving for Tokyo but first he had to go to the office for a while to settle unfinished business.

He could hear Wati's car honking outside. Halim knew the distinctive sound. Sofia was still in the bathroom. Halim rushed outside to open the gates and found Wati standing there with a thick coat over her arm. She was surprised to see Halim come out instead of Sofia but in any case she supposed that by now Halim would be well aware of Sofia's travel plans for Tokyo.

'This is for Sofia!' said Wati, handing the coat to Halim

through the still closed gates.

'Whose coat is this? Is it for Sofia?' Halim was baffled.

'It's mine. Sofia said she'd like to borrow it!'

'Wati, what's this coat for?'

'Sofia said she would like to borrow it for Tokyo. She didn't have time to buy one. Well, she's going along, isn't she?'

'She didn't tell me anything!'

'She probably wants to surprise you!' said Wati getting into her car.

Halim stood stunned by the locked gate. Wati's thick coat was hanging over his arm. He couldn't think straight. Was Sofia really expecting to go to Tokyo? How could it be that I did not know about it? Nora! Yes, Nora! How about Nora? She must be all packed to go!

'Halim!' He heard Sofia's voice at the door. 'Why are you standing by the gate!'

Halim turned. He was out of ideas and he felt as though his heart had stopped beating. He entered the house gingerly. He handed the thick coat to Sofia.

'Oh! Wati's coat! Let me try it on, I think it'll fit.' Sofia put on the coat. Halim looked on feeling empty and trying to hide his feelings. He was really surprised. It was not that Halim did not want Sofia to go. It was only that he faced a problem. The problem of Nora coming along.

If he had known this earlier, surely he could have put Nora off gently. But now it was too late. Nora was all ready and packed. Halim did not have the heart to disappoint Nora. Nora was not at fault because it was Halim who had invited her.

'Why do you look so troubled?' Sofia assumed that Wati had already told him she'd reserved two tickets instead of one.

'I've something to do at the office. I must go quickly.'

The Wife

Halim was afraid to face his wife. He was truly confused. He walked quickly to his car and Sofia went to the gate which was still locked. She knew that Halim was in a hurry. She opened the gates. Halim left without looking at Sofia, who was waiting to give him a smile.

'Are you really going with Halim to Tokyo?' asked Asmah, as she put on her white stockings. She was all ready with her nurse uniform to go to hospital.

Nora turned to Asmah. 'I wouldn't be lying, would I? Of course I'm going with Halim. When else will I get this golden chance to see another country. I've finished all my packing.'

'Nora, you still believe in men. It's not that you haven't been disappointed in the past. Haven't you learned your lesson yet?'

'What's so dangerous about Halim? I've been with him for long enough. If there's danger in Toky, there's also danger here!'

'Well, Nora, if he wasn't married, it'd be alright. But he's married with a grown up son.'

'Asmah, if he's willing to ask me to go with him to Tokyo, surely he's not just playing with me. If it was just all fun for him, why take the trouble to bring me to Tokyo? There're many Japanese women there, if he really wanted to fool around!'

'Ah, it's so difficult to talk to you Nora. You talk in circles. I say this, you say that. It gives me a headache!'

'Your job is to look after patients. You haven't got time

for headaches,' said Nora.

'Liaten, I wouldn't feel right if I didn't say anything. I'd feel responsible. But I do think that if a man has marriage in mind, he won't run around with you. If he runs around with you, that means that he's just fooling around. When he's done with you, he'll not want to get married anymore. Believe me!' Asmah moved toward the door.

'Halim's not that kind of man. He's different from the others!' Nora grabbed her handbag from the table and headed towards her car.

'I thought you'd taken holiday from work?' said Asmah.

'Yes, the plane leaves tonight but I want to go into town to get my hair done. I must change my hairstyle'

'O.K.! I'm leaving now.'

'What would you like from Tokyo?'

'Ah, don't get me anything! Your present to me is to take care of yourself!' said Asmah.

'Alright. Goodbye!' Nora waved as Asmah headed out.

I never thought I would be accompanying Halim to go to Tokyo, she thought. At first, I thought Halim was only joking as usual, but no, he was really serious.

I know one day he will ask me to marry him. I am younger than his wife and more attractive. But I don't want to share him with another wife. If he really loved me, he would leave Sofa.

Nora's car left the compound of her house. She turned toward the city. She knew Halim was crazy about her now.

Once he did run around with other women, but now there is just me. Odd, really odd, that Sofia manages to be patient after finding out that her husband is attracted to another woman. If it were me, I wouldn't let myself be embarrassed in such a way! If my husband did not want me, I would not want him either. Oh, this world is not that small.

Once, yes, when Zakaria left me, the world appeared small. Since then I've always been the one that leaves first. But with Halim it's different. I don't want to leave him. Ah! Even though he is someone's husband, what do I care? If his wife no longer loves him, why should they live under the same roof? I am baffled by the attitude of human beings who only pretend to be in love, when everyone already knows that power no longer binds the two of them. They are only subjected to the ties of marriage. That's all!

Sofia once said that she didn't want to live with pretense either, but isn't she pretending now? Sofia is afraid to tell Halim that she knows about our relationship! She is afraid that Halim will choose me!

Now Halim has chosen to take me to Tokyo and she doesn't even know about it. She doesn't know how her husband will embrace me in Tokyo. She won't know about anything, being stuck at home. Hmm! Let her take care of her beautiful home, let me take care of my beloved Halim.

Yes, Asmah is worried for me! She does not know -- perhaps we might get married there. Ah, let us marry first. Imagine Sofia's fury. Let her demand a divorce. I would not care, if she is silent, I will urge Halim to divorce her.

Still daydreaming, Nora arrived at the saloon. She wanted to look more beautiful and attractive so that Halim would completely forget his wife. Soon Halim would marry her. Nora stepped out of the car beaming.

'You're not working today?' asked Rahim as he sipped the hot soup. He felt fresh after a short nap.

'No,' answered Malisa briefly, as she poured something into the glass.

'Isn't today a working day?'

'I worked last night. Rokiah and I work different shifts. She's in administration. I'm in the I.T. department. Sometimes, I have to work until the early hours. If I'm on the late shift, I'll not be working the next day.' Malisa spooned rice onto Rahim's plate.

'Well, I was quite surprised when I saw rice on the table when I came out of the room. When I got here, no one was home.'

'Oh, earlier I went to the junction to buy fish. If I'm not working, I cook early so that at night I can relax and there's no need to cook anymore, only heat things up. Today there's a good show on TV, I don't want to miss it.'

Rahim smiled. The girl with the dimples was still very young. 'Lisa, will you eat with me? I feel embarrassed to dine alone.'

'I'm used to eating alone. Rokiah never eats at home. Wati never eats. Sometimes they have dinner first before coming home. And then they go straight to bed. I feel sorry for them at times. They work too hard,' said Malisa as she spooned more rice onto the plate.

'Hmm *percik* fish!'

'Fresh fish, it's best to make *percik*, if it has been frozen for some time, it's good for curry,' said Malisa giving the

98

fish dish to Rahim.'I was quite surprise to see the Mercedes so early this morning,' she continued. 'Usually you arrive in the evening.'

'Yes, I'm on leave for two days. My body feels really exhausted. At first I had a cold. And then, it was alright for a while. Now, the cold is back. The doctor gave me two days off.'

'Oh, you're not well! No wonder when I entered the house, it was silent. There's a car outside, but everything's silent.'

'I took some medicine, something that made me sleepy.'

Malisa looked sympathetic. 'Drink lots of water and rest. If you don't rest, the fever won't go away.' She handed the vegetable dish of salad to Rahim.

'Where're you from Malisa?'.

'Not far from here, Kampung Serindik.'

'So, are there lots of crickets there?' Rahim was smiling now.

'Why are you smiling?'

'It's nothing.'

'Hmm, you purposely don't want to tell me ... that's not fair,' said Malisa. She stopped eating.

'Please, continue eating. Don't stop. Actually, I was thinking of a bird I caught when I was little,' said Rahim trying to explain himself.

'You like to keep birds?'

'Yes!'

'At our house in the village, there were so many birds. My grandfather really loved birds. We even had ones that could talk,' she said.

'Is that right?' Rahim really did love birds. He also used to have a bird that could talk. 'What did it say?'

'Oh, it always called out, 'Lisa! Lisa! Good morning'. When I came home, it became really excited.'

Rahim laughed. 'If others came, surely it'd say the same thing, even though it could be evening.'

Malisa smiled. 'Have more soup before it gets cool. It's good for that cold.'

At first, Rahim wanted to protest but Malissa poured the soup before he could protest, so he was forced to finish it.

'Would you like coffee or tea? The mung bean porridge is ready,' said Malisa, as she got up to go to the kitchen.

'Mung bean porridge! Well, I'll not refuse.'

'Right! I already knew that!' said Malisa as she turned to Rahim who was still at the dining table.

'Have you waited for me long at home?' asked Wati as the Mercedes drove out of Seroja Road.

'Wati, didn't I call you yesterday to inform you that I would be on leave today? My body is aching, so the doctor gave me sick leave. I didn't feel like staying in Kaloi so I arrived at your house at about eleven o'clock this morning,' said Rahim.

'So what did you do the whole day at home?'.

'I slept, what else. I feel a bit better now,' said Rahim. 'Where are we going?'

'Oh, sorry I forgot to explain. We're going to the airport. This evening Sofia and Halim are leaving for Tokyo. I wanted to ask Sofia to get me a few things.'

'You're always buying things!'

'Well, the cream that I bought in Tokyo is finished. They don't sell it here. Sofia doesn't know which one it is. That's why I've brought an empty container so that it'll be easier for her to buy it there.'

'Well, it's fortunate that Malaysian men haven't started using face cream—if not life would be really complicated!'

Wati was silent for a while. She appeared to be deep in thought.

'What's wrong, Wati; what's on your mind?' asked Rahim, as he shifted gear.

'Do you know that Halim only learned today that his wife's going with him to Tokyo,' said Wati.

'How's that?'

'I don't know what's wrong with them both. Hmm, Halim hasn't changed his promiscuous ways. I thought I was paving the way for them to have a second honeymoon in Tokyo. It's better to bring your wife than another woman. But Halim came to my office wanting to know why Sofia had changed her mind whereas she had really wanted to go from the beginning. Halim knew only at the last minute that Sofia would be going with him.'

'Well, so what if Sofia changed her mind? You and I always make our plans last minute.'

'Yes,' said Wati. 'I know that you're always in a hurry to make decisions. We got married as fast as lightning; my family didn't even have time to prepare anything. If you've made up your mind, you cannot wait till next day.'

'I don't know Halim that well. Is he a womaniser?'

'Well, when you are attractive and have money, you're bound to have many admirers.'

'I'm amazed that you were not one of Halim's admirers

at university.'

'I had my own admirers...'

'Or victims,' Rahim interrupted.

Wati laughed heartily. 'But I shouldn't complain ... otherwise I'd have lost my chance,' added Rahim.

'I hope Halim doesn't misbehave in Tokyo,' said Wati.

'Misbehave how?'

'Are you really so naive? If you'd been to Tokyo, you'd know what I mean.'

Without realising it, they had arrived at the airport.

As always, it was packed with people but they could see Sofia standing alone by a trolley of luggage. She appeared to be waiting for something. Halim was nowhere to be seen.

He said he wanted to change some currency and asked me to wait here, thought Sofia. If I move away from this place, it would be rather difficult for him to find me. But Wati also said that she would be coming. There is something she wants me to buy. Ah, let Wati look for me: if I look for her, and she looks for me, it would only waste time.

Wati and Rahim held hands as they walked towards the departure hall. Wati stopped at a place where there were many people waiting to depart. She squeezed Rahim's hand tightly. Rahim also stopped.

'What's wrong, Wati?'

'Oh no! Not this!' The words spilled out of Wati's mouth unconsciously. Her eyes were fixed on the busy crowd in front of her.

'Wati!' said Rahim, 'What's wrong?'

'Can you believe, that's Nora, the one with the jacket and red pants. From all those bags she's carrying, it looks as if she's going abroad!'

'What's wrong with her going abroad?' asked Rahim looking at the woman with brown curly hair.

'She thinks people will not recognise her with the dyed hair and dark sunglasses—no way!' said Wati getting angry.

'Why are you angry with her?'

'Don' t you get it? That's Nora. She's extremely intimate with Halim. Where is she going with those bags and thick coat?'

'Eh, are you just going to stand here?' asked Rahim.

'Wait!' Her eyes were still on Nora. 'Wait, look at that!'

Rahim looked over to see a man was approaching Nora.

'Rahim, there's Halim! See that? He's with Nora.'

'What's wrong with that?'

'Halim is Sofia's husband. What else are they planning now? Where's Nora going?'

'Why does it bother you so much? That's their business, isn't it?'

'Ah, you don't understand!' said Wati.

'Let's go over there if you really want to find out; we'll ask them.'

'Oh, no, Rahim, I don't want him to know that I know.' Pulling her husband by the hand, she moved away from Halim and Nora and then a moment later she spotted Sofia. Now Wati understood why Halim had been so worried by the last minute news that Sofia wanted to accompany him.

'Wati!' said Sofia. 'I thought you weren't coming at all.'

'I'm a bit late,' said Wati.

'Halim has gone over to the foreign exchange.'

It's wives he wants to exchange, Wati thought silently. She felt bitter, but forced a smile.

'Sofia, you haven't met my husband, Rahim. Rahim, this

is Sofia, my best friend from childhood.'

Sofia held out her hand to Rahim. 'How are you?'

'I'm fine,' said Rahim, as he shook Sofia's soft hand. 'When is departure time?'

'About eight, I guess,'

'Hmm, soon.' Rahim looked at his watch 'How long will you be there?'

'Not long, one week, I think.'

Wati kept turning over in her mind what she had just seen. She could hardly believe it.... Ah, it's better that I wait until they board, she thought. If Nora was truly going along, she would presumbly board the same airplane. Let me wait, and in fewer than fifteen minutes I will know the truth. Wati looked at Sofia's cheerful face and her heart felt bitter remorse beyond words. Sofia appeared so happy, so let Sofia be happy as long as possible. People said that as long as one was in a state of ignorance.

'Wati, didn't you say you wanted me to get you some cream?' Sofia reminded Wati, who was quiet and lost in thought.

'Oh yes, I almost forgot.' Wati produced an empty container from her handbag. 'Here! If it's any trouble, don't worry. I'll try some other time.'

'Come on, it's no bother,' said Sofia. 'Ah, there's Halim.'

Rahim said hello and held out his hand and Halim shook it. He appeared calm. He smiled at them all. 'Wati!' he said.

Wati only nodded. She was trying her best to hide her feelings. She was tired of men who cheated on their wives. It hadn't mattered so much when Halim was without responsibilities and family, but now he was married, with a good position. Why must he behave like an idiot! Wati tried to stop thinking but the more she resisted, the faster her thoughts came through, and the angrier she felt.

'Ah, they're calling you now,' Rahim said. 'Better go, otherwise you'll be rushing.'

'O.K., goodbye,' said Halim holding his hand out to Rahim. He saw that Wati looked withdrawn and uncommunicative. 'Wati, we're leaving now,' said Halim.

Wati forced a smile. Barely.

'Goodbye, Wati.' Sofia held out her hand.

'See you soon,' said Wati gripping Sofia's hand anxiously. She was worried about her friend, guilty because she was the one who had urged Sofia to go along.

Halim and Sofia walked through the departure gate toward the waiting plane. Wati didn't take her eyes off the brown haired woman in the red pants. She saw Nora among the others departing for Tokyo with Halim and Sofia and gripped Rahim's hand. Rahim felt the piercing of Wati's long fingernails. She was still looking at the people who were walking toward the main entrance. It was as if she was though in another world, not conscious of her surroundings.

'Wati,' said Rahim, 'do you want to stay here longer?'

'Let's go.' Wati turned toward Rahim still feeling furious. She hadn't expected that to happen. How could Halim cheat on his wife, and not even hide it. The office people were right about Halim's wife not suspecting anything. Poor Sofia.

Nora was angry beyond words. Men could not be trusted at all. They said one thing but meant another. If I'd known this, I would never have followed him to Tokyo. What is his reason for bringing his wife along? Perhaps he wants to show off to me what a good husband he would be. Maybe he wants to give me an idea how he would behave with me as his wife. He was whispering to his wife as if they were on honeymoon—but Sofia has no idea that this is a lunar eclipse!

If he wants to have a second honeymoon with his wife, why does he have to drag me along? Why should I follow like a mangy dog!

Nora tried to focus on the magazine she was holding. The man beside her glanced over two or three times. But she ignored him. Once in a while, her eyes teared up. She wiped them quickly, fearing that the man might notice.

Asmah was right, thought Nora; she was truly right. She told me not to be intimate with a married man, but I did not pay heed. I thought Halim was different from others, but now what has happened?

When he invited me to Tokyo, it felt like the world was mine. He sets aside his wife and wants to take me with him, which means that he loves me more. Hah! hah! That was only my assumption. The man has a forked tongue. Who is he with now if not his beloved wife?

Sofia! Sofia! Do not think that you have won. You don't know who I am. You think I am petite and therefore fear you? Hah! I fear no one. Sofia knows about my relationship with her husband. I will bring it into the open no matter what happens. I won't admit defeat. Halim will have to choose between the two of us, Sofia or me. No matter what Halim thinks, it is better to have an eclipse of the moon rather than an eclipse of the heart!

In the darkness of the night, the plane moved smoothly

toward its destination. Nora felt her life was without direction. She drifted lost above a shoreless ocean.

Wati was lying on the bed staring at the ceiling, lost in her thoughts. Rahim was playing with the soft hair on her forehead. 'Your thoughts seem to have left with the aeroplane earlier' he said.

'Rahim, I feel sorry for Sofia. She has no idea that Halim has brought Nora along with them to Tokyo.'

'There's nothing you can do. The plane's already far from here....'

'Yes, I know I can't do anything but I feel the hurt, the insult.'

'Why should you feel the insult?'

'I'm a woman, I know the feelings of a woman cheated by her beloved husband.'

'I trust that Halim loves his wife,' said Rahim.

'If he loves Sofia then why did he bring another woman along? I know Nora has been pursuing Halim. She even gets jealous of me if she sees me with Halim!'

'Perhaps Halim is attracted to you, that's why she's jealous!' Rahim teased.

Wati smiled. She knew that Rahim was trying to make her feel better. She leaned over and touched his hair where it fell onto his forehead, as she gazed at Rahim's handsome features.

'Why do you look at me like that?' asked Rahim. His forefinger was touching the middle of Wati's forehead. He ran the finger along Wati's nose.

Wati took hold of his hand. 'Rahim, how could he have cheated his wife? How could he divide his love?'

Her husband shook his head. 'Despite that, I still believe that he loves his wife. Perhaps that Nora pursued him. She must relent.'

'But if his love is deep enough, how could it change so quickly? I know that he's a womaniser but I thought that once married, he would be loyal to his wife! I'm lucky that you're not like that. If secretly you are then what can I do?'

'What if you're like that?' asked Rahim.

'I had my good time in university!'

'That was why you couldn't find a steady boyfriend then. Everyone was running scared!' Rahim laughed.

'Poor you, falling into my snare!' She took hold of his hands and squeezed them tightly.

'But if the snare is a golden one, and the princess that set the trap is alluring, then I'm willing to be trapped,' said Rahim. He released his hands from Wati's firm hold. He could see that she had finally forgotten about Sofia and Halim somewhre far away in the sky. Her thoughts were focused back on the earth, on the husband whom she loved so very dearly.

8

WHEN Sofia opened her eyes, she saw that food had already been laid on the small table in the room. She could hear Halim singing hoarsely in the bathroom. When he was younger, Halim used to sing on stage in the village whenever there was a ceremony. Ah! That was the past ... But in the old days, I would never have got the chance to come to Japan. I cannot believe it, thought Sofia, I cannot believe all this is really happening. Wati was right, a second honeymoon could make our love grow fresh again. I feel younger, I feel different when I am alone with Halim like this, far from my own country, far from everyone I know, just the two of us.

Halim's voice was silent. So was the water in the bathroom. Sofia turned to look at Halim as he walked back into the bedroom drying his hair.

'Is the Princess up?' asked Halim.

Sofia smiled.

'Isn't it cold?' she said.

'Eh, hot water, power shower,' said Halim. 'Let's eat, the eggs will get cold.'

Sofia smiled again. She had never before received such treatment from her husband. She got up and approached the small table. Halim was all ready in pants and shirt, about to take some toast. Sofia sat on a chair beside him.

'Hmm, that looks delicious!' she said.

'Yes, it really is,' said Halim, pouring coffee into Sofia's cup. 'So… how's Tokyo?'

'I don't know, I haven't seen anything yet.'

'This morning I have some work to do, then after lunch I'll take you to see the city.'

'Will you be back for lunch?'

'Yes, I'll be back. We can dine downstairs or we can eat in the city.'

'Whatever is good!'

After finishing a piece of bread and a cup of coffee, Halim reached for his bag and coat and left. He closed the door behind him and noted the number, which was 2010. He took the elevator to level five, got out and turned left. He stopped at door number 5142. He placed the bag at the door and knocked. He knocked a few times. His heart was pounding too. Was no one inside? Halim knocked again.

At last the door opened. Halim went straight in.

'Good morning,' he said. 'Have you had breakfast?'

Nora was silent, refusing to answer. She pretended to clean up the room. She folded the blanket and arranged the pillows.

Halim went directly to the telephone and telephoned for coffee and toast with eggs to be sent to room 5142. After he placed the telephone back on its receiver, he sat on a chair next to the small table. He studied Nora who was all made up. But Nora still refused to talk. Halim felt guilty.

'Nora, you know, I never expected something like this to happen. You understand, don't you? I had no idea she was coming. It turned out Madam Fatimawati had booked the ticket for her.'

Nora was still furious beyond words. She began to pack her clothes into her bag. This was not what she had planned.

She never imagined that she would face such a situation. However, she was not giving up, not at all. Perhaps Halim was also disappointed to bring along his beloved wife when he had expected to have a holiday with his lover.

'So what's your plan now?' asked Nora.

'As before!' said Halim.

'How is that possible?'

'Ah, don't you worry about that. Leave it to me. I know how to take care of things.'

There was a knock on the door and Halim got up to answer it. He took the food tray from a young Japanese man in a red jacket.

Nora was already at the table. She had begun to cool down. If Halim did not love her, he would not have taken the trouble to have breakfast with her. Nora even began to smile. Halim placed the tray on the table. Nora sat on a chair near the table. She poured coffee for Halim and then for herself. Next, she added sugar and milk.

'Hmm, hot toast,' said Halim. He buttered a slice and placed it on Nora's plate. Halim had never served her. She felt proud to receive this special treatment.

'You're not eating?' Nora asked.

'Eh, who could resist hot toast like this,' said Halim. He buttered another piece of toast. Earlier he'd eaten only one slice of toast in Sofia's room. Now he was eating another slice in Nora's room. He smiled.

'When does the conference start?' asked Nora.

'10.30 in the morning. I suppose lunch will be provided, so if you need lunch, just call downstairs, alright?' said Halim.

Nora was silent.

'Or maybe you'd like to look around at the shops, but I

cannot accompany you. This is the first day, so I'll be a bit busy. But wait for me at 7.00 o'clock and we'll go out for dinner. Where would you like to go? To a night club? A secluded seafood restaurant?'

Nora was truly ecstatic. She had not expected Halim to take her to a night club or indeed anywhere.

'Ah, I don't have anything to wear for a nightclub,' she said.

'That's not a problem.' Halim put his hand into his pocket. He took out some American dollars. 'Go downstairs. In the lobby, there are all types of shops; choose whichever outfit you like. Japanese currency is too confusing. Just take these American dollars. They'll accept them.'

Halim put the money on the table next to the cup of coffee.

'Think about where you'd like to go tonight. I'll call you in the afternoon but don't worry if you're out sightseeing – just leave a note at the counter.' He paused, 'Or better not, it might be given to Sofia. We'll just agree that I'll meet you at seven tonight. Wait for me in your room.'

'O.K.' Nora smiled.

'I've got to go now; enjoy your shopping.'

'Thank you.'

'Goodbye!' Halim reached for his briefcase and coat, and left.

Walking down the corridor, Halim felt truly relieved. He'd hardly slept at all the previous night, lying awake and worrying about what to do. This first day should run smoothly now. Sofia would have her lunch here, or in town, and then he would go sightseeing with her until she felt tired. By the time he knew she would have a headache and would not want to go out anymore that night. In the evening he would go dancing with Nora at the Hiroshima Hotel. It was all settled. Now he could study the conference proposal in peace.

Even though Sofia was exhausted, she could not sleep. She had been all over the city today with Halim, until she felt that she could not take another step.

Tokyo was a huge city, congested with traffic and people. There were many beautiful things, but life here was expensive. Sofia tried to close her eyes but could not. She just lay in bed looking at the hotel room ceiling.

Halim said he had a dinner event. It was already two in the morning, but he had still not returned. Eating should only take one hour, if there were speeches, it would take another hour. If the dinner began at eight o'clock, surely it would have finished at ten or eleven. If the dinner began at nine, surely it would have finished at eleven or twelve.

Maybe the journey from there to here took two hours. Maybe ... maybe ... thought Sofia. There were all kinds of stories about what went on in Tokyo. Sofia tried not to think of all them, but she could not help herself. Her mind was spinning and she could not stop it.

Sofia reached for the newspaper on the small table next to the bed. She began reading and after a short while finally fell asleep.

Some time later, Sofia woke up. Her wristwatch showed 3.10 in the morning. Halim was still not back.

Calm down! Calm down! thought Sofia. Try to think

positively, don't think about negative things, don't think about unhappy things. It was Halim's choice to bring me here. He could have left me behind but he brought me along. If he wanted to fool around, he would not have asked me to come. But he did ask me to come here, that is a fact. If he had not wanted to invite me to go with him, I would surely never have got to see the land of the rising sun.

People say that Japanese wives are always smiling even if their husbands arrive home late. Could it be that he has brought me here to learn how to become like those Japanese wives who are always patient and obedient to their husbands. Perhaps, he wants me to smile always even if my heart is unhappy.

Enough, enough, enough! Sofia warned her mind. This trip was a good thing. How did it change to something bad? Enough! Don't think other than what is good ... Halim brought me here because he wanted me with him, even though at times he is forced to stay out until the early morning.

Sofia turned to her right. Her eyelids were beginning to feel heavy again. She closed them and fell into a slumber.

When Sofia opened her eyes, she found Halim had been and gone. Breakfast was ready on the table next to the bed. Halim had obviously eaten. There were cigarette butts on the tray beside the empty cup.

Sofia got up, but her head was spinning because of lack of sleep. She saw that Halim's bed was not made up. His clothes and a wet towel were strewn about.

Sofia looked at her wristwatch, which showed that it was already after nine in the morning. Ah, how could I have overslept. She knew the coffee would be getting cold but she was too lazy to get up. Her body felt exhausted.

Sofia lifted her pillow and propped it up against the headboard. She leaned on the pillow, trying to think. What happened? Oh yes, yesterday I arrived back late from going to a show with Halim, then we went to dinner. She had no idea what time they rhad eached the hotel. Around two perhaps.

Her feelings of exhaustion were balanced by feelings of contentment. Now she knew what Tokyo looked like at night. No wonder Halim loved coming back late. An indescribale happiness was aflame in her heart. Even though her body was tired, she was happy, contented that she no longer doubted Halim. Now she understood that Halim needed to follow the wishes of his Japanese partners. As a guest, it was not proper for him to refuse their invitations or the programmes of hospitality that they had prepared for him.

Sofia got up and walked towards the bathroom. Even though her head felt heavy, Sofia tried to recall all the events of the previous day. Sofia had never felt this happy. She had never recieved such special treatment from her husband.

Halim ... oh Halim, what will happen to me without him, what would happen to me if he left me...?

Enough! Enough! Haven't I said that I do not want to think of negative things! I only want to think of good things. Sofia tried to think of the red silk which she saw at the big department store. If I like the material, Halim will surely buy it for me, but wait, I want to see others first. Perhaps I will find something better.

The coffee was cold, the eggs were cold, the toast was cold and hard. But if the heart is content, everything tastes delicious and Sofia enjoyed her cold breakfast. As she ate she remembered that only two days ago she had been so angry because Halim returned late; now all that anger was finished with. Perhaps, she had passed the first test, which was to always smile even when her husband came home late.

When Halim was working, Sofia often read poetry in the hotel room. She bought plenty of Japanese magazines and novels. Sometimes, the TV also aired nice shows. She learned about Japanese cooking and a little bit about their life there.

Feeling pleased with life, Sofia decided to go down for a walk. She had noticed an interesting clothes store situated near the hotel lobby.

Halim is really good at making excuses! If there are formal invitations, I need to bring my wife. Well, if he really wanted to, he could do anything. If Halim really wanted to bring me to any invited events, he could; the Japanese here don't know who his wife is.

He could introduce me as his wife and all the problems would be over. There's no need to hide me whenever he meets his Japanese friends. Halim should have introduced me as his wife from the beginning, so it would be easy or us to go anywhere.

Halim is purposely showing off to be like the Japanese. The Japanese have only one wife, he wants to show that he has only one wife. What now? I am constantly left behind because he is forced to bring his wife to attend the invited events.

Ah, I am bored! I do not want to be imprisoned, even in a hotel this big. Why must he be afraid? His wife already knows about me! Why this need for secrecy? Hah! I've been patient far too long. When the volcano erupts, the effects will be truly devastating. But everybody has their limits. For me, the limit of my patience is here. From now on, I don't care who sees me. What's there to be embarrassed about? If Halim fears showing his love to me openly, let me do it. For Sofia, the truth matters, and my relationship with Halim is her problem. She has told me so. So why should I worry about it? For a long while I didn't want Halim to know that Sofia knows, because I understand Halim, a man who fears his wife.

I was afraid that he would leave me because he feared his wife and adult son.

But now I need no longer be afraid. I will expose the truth because after all this is what Sofia wanted. She said once she did not want to live in pretence.

Alright Sofia, if that is what you want, I will give it to you. I will show you and Halim the reality which he himself does not want to face.

Nora had been looking at the magazine in her hands. With her brown curly hair and big sunglasses, who would know that she was Nora, dressed in a swimming suit and lying beside the swimming pool.

Two more days left, thought Nora. After that, we will all leave for home. I need to expose the truth to Halim and Sofia before we return. This is my only chance. Otherwise, when? This is the time for Halim to prove his love for me.

Sofia is not the only one who wants the truth. If he truly loves me, I will know it then.

That evening Halim invited Nora for dinner. When he arrived at Nora's room, he was shocked to see Nora without her curly brown locks, but straight hair, like before. She was also not wearing a western outfit but a kebaya with a tight sarong, showing off her beautiful body.

Halim's initial shock subsided when Nora explained to him that no one knew her in Tokyo. Furthermore, they would be leaving soon.

That evening, Nora only wanted to spend time at the night club on the eleventh floor of the hotel. After dinner they danced.

Sofia ate on her own that night. Only bread. She was tired of Japanese food. Besides, there was nothing exciting about eating alone.

Shortly, there was a telephone call from the reception counter. The Japanese woman told Sofia that Halim was waiting for her at the Nagasaki Palace nightclub on the eleventh floor. Quickly, Sofia put on her clothes. After dinner Halim and his friends had a dancing party, perhaps Halim forgot to inform her that wives were also invited.

On the eleventh floor, Sofia was greeted by a Japanese hostess wearing a kimono. She followed her into the Nagasaki Palace.

The place was rather dim. There were only flickering lights here and there. The band was playing a slow number, romantic and somehow nostalgic.

The hostess in the kimono led her to table number 20. The chairs were empty but there were two glasses filled with some sort of alcoholic drink. Sofia recognized Halim's cigarettes and lighter. There was a golden purse on the table. Sofia asked the woman in a kimono where Halim was, and the woman pointed towards a couple dancing to the slow music.

Sofia gasped. For a moment it felt as her heart had stopped beating. Sofia summoned the hostess again. She wanted to know who had asked her there. Was it the woman in Halim's embrace or was it Halim himself? After receiving an answer from the Japanese hostess, Sofia approached table number 20.

Nora, Nora, you are forever hauting me! It turns out that you are on our honeymoon with us. Now what is your plan in calling me here? You want to show me that Halim has brought you to Tokyo as well? And you also want to rub Halim's nose in this problem, so that he is forced to choose between you and me. All this while Halim is floating, not knowing which direction to choose. Now by bringing me here, you think that Halim will be forced to decide?

Nora, you are immature, still trying to throw bait in the deep ocean. Nora, I am used to the waves and storms. If you want to show your strength, why hide your talons?

Sofia smirked: her lips were forming a smile even though her heart was injured. It is not that I am angry with Halim, it is not that I am not disappointed. In reality, I am already experiencing that silently. But God is with me. I am not afraid, but if I was brought here only to break my heart and make me feel small, I am willing to bear everything even though the things are are happening are not my fault. God protects those who are not wrong. God is on the right side.

I do not want to think about Halim, about how crushed my heart feels at the moment, but I will face this petite woman who calls herself a Muslim, who is willing to lower the dignity of her own kind in public such as this.

She wants me to show my anger, my loathing, my fury because she is with my husband. Huh, if Halim desires love as cheap as that, that is his business. I do not want to be humiliated in front of everyone like this.

Dear God, give me the strength to face this woman.

The soft music ended and Sofia steeled herself to look cheerful. She had never been a good actor but this time she must face the challenge.

Halim and Nora walked hand in hand toward their table. At first Halim did not see Sofia, but then he started. The usually cheerful face became deadly pale. How had Sofia known where he was?

Halim was shocked into silence. What excuse could he have? What could he possibly say? Oh! God, how had this happened? This was truly unexpected, impossible. Impossible!

'Hello Nora!' said Sofia, ignoring Halim.

Now Halim was even more surprised. Sofia knew Nora? He realised that his body was trembling all over.

'I'm sorry Halim, I know tonight is Nora's turn, but Mr Sukiyomo telephoned me in the room earlier. He said we're to go to the Kyoto Hotel. They're all waiting for us there. There's a special show,' said Sofia.

Nora and Halim sat facing Sofia. Sofia tried not to show her feelings. However, her heart was pounding. Her feet were cold.

Nora's face was subdued, no longer confident of victory. 'But I'm sorry, Nora, Mr Sukiyomo did not invite you

120

along; he said only Mr Halim and wife,' continued Sofia.

Halim looked at Nora and saw that she was about to burst into tears.

Sofia got up, 'If you want to come along, Halim, it's up to you. After all it must be more exciting to embrace this little woman than watch a show at the Kyoto Hotel.' She reached for her purse from the table.

Halim was still stunned.

'If you don't want to come, Halim, it's alright, I'll just go back to the room and call Mr Sukiyomo to let him know that you're exhausted tonight.'

Halim really wanted Sofia to leave first, so that he could explain to Nora, before going with Sofia. But Sofia was faster to act. She got up, held out her hand to Halim. Halim was forced to take her hand and get up.

'O.K., Nora? If I can come here all by myself, I'm sure you can find your way back to your room, or any other room.' Now Sofia was showing her anger. She felt she couldn't help it.

Nora still had not said a word. She was shocked, confused. This was not what she had planned. It was not Sofia who was crying upon finding out about her cheating husband; it was she herself who was in tears. She stayed sitting stunned at the table as Sofia and Halim left.

Halim did not know what to say, did not know what to do. Sofia was silent but her face was red. Halim realised that Sofia was furious, but what could he do? This was not part of his plan. He never expected this to happen.

The door of the elevator opened. Sofia and Halim walked in. The door closed. Sofia pressed number 2. Halim was bewildered. If they were to go to Kyoto Hotel, G should be pressed. But he remained quiet. Perhaps Sofia wanted to take something from the room before they left. He did not dare to speak, just in case he said something wrong. Sofia held the helm, let her steer. Sofia was also silent and she paid no attention to Halim beside her. To her Halim was like a shadow. The floor 2 light lit up. The elevator door opened, Sofia walked out. She didn't care if Halim came out or not. But Halim followed Sofia, not knowing what else he should do.

Sofia headed towards the room. Halim was behind her. Was it true that Mr Sukiyomo wanted them to go to Kyoto Hotel? Was this just Sofia's ploy? Halim did not dare ask.

Sofia opened the door with the key in her hand and immediately tried to close it behind her, nearly hitting Halim on the nose. Then she sat on a chair, her face red and serious. Halim knew that when Sofia was really furious, she would not cry. His mind was racing fast with all sorts of thoughts. He wondered if he should keep quiet, without doing anything.

Halim knew that he was guilty but he did not know how to explain the truth. He saw no way out of the trap which he himself had set. He observed Sofia as she sat frozen in the chair. Her stares pierced the wall of the room.

'Sofia...!' Halim began to face reality. He had to do something.

Sofia was silent. She ignored Halim calling out to her.

'Sofia...,' Halim repeated.

'Halim.' Sofia turned to Halim. Her eyes were looking at him sharply. 'There are no words that can describe my feelings now. I feel small, extremely small. I feel humiliated, extremely humiliated.'

Halim went nearer to Sofia. He tried to carress her hair.

'Don't touch me!' yelled Sofia.

122

The Wife

Halim froze in his step, 'Sofia...'

'Don't touch me! If you treat me in the same way as that other whore, I'm also filthy, you have besmirched me!' Sofia closed her eyes. Her heart was pounding. 'How could you put filth on the purity that I have given you...,' she added. 'How could a husband do such a thing to his own wife, even if he hated that wife?'

'I don't hate you!' said Halim.

'If you don't hate me, hah, how could you treat me in the same way as that whore!'

'Sofia, forgive me, forgive me...'

'Halim, look at me. See these eyes looking at you, perhaps this is the last time you will do so. You're aware that I cannot love a husband who has cheated on me. Don't even think that I'll continue to love you after you've humiliated me in such a way; from this moment, my love for you is dead. You've soiled it with your sin. From now onwards, I'm a wife without a heart, without feelings, without love. I'm only a wife, a wife who is obedient to her husband, a wife who will just say yes to everything without protest. I'm a wife with an empty soul, whose love is dead. My love is buried here.' Sofia buried her face in her two hands and sobbed.

'Sofia, I don't want to lose your love. I need your love...' said Halim, taking Sofia's hand in his. Sofia did not protest at Halim's touch. She had made the oath of being an obedient wife but she knew that she could not force herself to love him again. Her heart was crushed.

'Sofia, look at me, say that you still love me!' Halim pleaded.

'Not now, now my love is all gone. Now my heart is empty. You do what you like. I return you back to yourself, for you to take care of your own self physically and mentally. I don't want to know about your sins, those you have to bear yourself.'

Halim could not say anything else. He was without words. His heart felt sad and touched. It was unexpected, beyond his thoughts. 'Maybe, one day you'll love me as you used to?'

'That rests entirely on you!'

'Meaning?'

'Meaning; I don't know. From this moment, I live without hope. I accept whatever that comes. I face every challenge. Every day that passes ... every moment that I experience, I'll face it bravely. Only God will guide me through this alone, without holding on to anything, without support from anyone. I live only for God and my children!' Sofia sobbed again. Tears ran down her cheeks.

'What about me? Don't I mean anything to you now?'

'You haven't needed my love for a long time. You, for a while now probably, have tried to seek other love. I hope you find what you're looking for. For me, my love is dead. Perhaps it'll never live again.'

'Sofia ... how could you...' He placed his head on Sofia's lap, as he sobbed.

'Forgive me, Halim, I've tried my best. After this, I could only give my body without my soul.' She allowed her husband to bury his head in her lap. She still wanted to caress Halim's head like she used to. She wanted to coax him, but she sat stiffly, without doing anything.

'Halim, I'm leaving tomorrow.'

Halim looked up. He didn't want her to leave like this. 'But my work is still not done...'

'I didn't ask you to return. I'll wait for you at home.'

said Sofia.

9

THE plane had landed. Sofia got up from her seat. All through the journey she had cried without stopping and felt the aching of her heart.

She followed the trail of passengers down the plane's high steps onto the earth of her homeland, the beloved Malaysia of her birth. Sofia wiped away the tears that flowed again from beneath her dark sunglasses. Slowly she followed the other passengers towards the terminal.

The scarf that was tied at her neck was waving, blown by the aircraft's fan. She adjusted the cloth.

After going through customs, Sofia found herself in the packed airport terminal looking around for a taxi.

'Sofia!' She heard a voice calling.

Sofia stopped. She turned around.

'Wati!'

'Sofia!' Wati was calling out as she ran towards her. Wati had expected this. Wati knew that something would happen.

'Wati!' Sofia could not stop the tears from falling. She hugged Wati tightly as she cried in sobs.

'Sofia ... Sofia, calm down. Let's leave now,' said Wati, caressing Sofia's hair.

'I never thought, I never thought...!'

People around them were staring.

'Let's leave this place.' Wati took Sofia's trolley and steered her friend towards the car. Sofia followed, without a word.

When they reached the white BMW, Sofia stopped and her hand touched Wati's, 'I don't want to go home,' she said.

'Where would you like to go?'

'Anywhere...'

Wati put Sofia's luggage into the boot of the car and then opened the door. 'Get in,' she said.

They both sat in silence for a moment and then Wati turned to her friend. 'Why did you come back without Halim?'

'I couldn't bear to be there another day,' said Sofia. 'How did you know I was arriving tonight?'

'Halim called me to come and pick you up. I have to call him back to say that you've arrived.'

'Don't bother, don't call; he doesn't care if I live or die!' said Sofia, furious.

Wati started the car engine and drove off.

'Sofia, you don't have to hide what Halim has done; there's no need to defend his dignity. I'm your real friend and I also know what Halim has done. I saw Nora get on that plane to Tokyo with the two of you,' said Wati.

'You saw?' asked Sofia, 'Then why didn't you tell me?'

'I wanted you to be happy with Halim. As long as you didn't know, I thought you would be happy,' said Wati, turning her car left.

'Yes that's true. At first, I thought I was in a dream world with my beloved husband. Hah!' Sofia laughed aloud. 'Beloved husband. Hah!' She laughed again.

'Calm down, Sofia,' said Wati. 'Be patient.' She squeezed Sofia's right hand.

'Yes, Wati, I truly never expected it. Even till the last minute, I didn't know. Halim took care of me like a princess.

I opened my eyes, there was food. He took me shopping, chose what I wanted, paid for everything. At night, his friends entertained us with all kinds of Japanese shows. We went everywhere.'

'I only found out at the last minute and even then it was not from Halim, but from Nora. She'd got someone to call me saying Halim was waiting. Actually, she wanted me to discover her embracing Halim at the night club. She wanted me to see Halim's reaction. She thought I would cry, and plead! But this is Sofia. Don't try to fool around with Sofia!'

'What did you do?' Wati signaled and turned right. Her face was apprehensive.

'I waited at the table until they finished dancing. When Halim got to the table, he was unbelievably shocked. He didn't say a word. I was the only one talking.'

'What did you say?'

'Hmm! If Nora can concoct a lie, I can do it ten times better. When they approached the table, I greeted Nora first. Halim was shocked!'

Wati was also surprised; she'd had no idea that Sofia knew about Nora.

'You knew Nora?'

'Yes!'

'You knew about their affair?'

'Yes,'

Wati was silent. This was unexpected.'And then, what happened?' she asked.

'I was trembling all over but I prayed to God for courage to face the challenge. I said, forgive me Halim, I know tonight is Nora's turn ... but Mr Sukiyomo called inviting Mr Halim and wife to the Kyoto Hotel. There's a show there, and they're all waiting for us. Sorry Nora, you're not invited, I said. After that I got up, held out my hand to Halim. He had to take my hand, or he would have looked bad, because everyone saw me standing and holding out my hand.'

'What did Nora say?'

'Nora didn't say anything. I was furious. I vented my anger on her too,' added Sofia.

'What did you say?'

'I said, if I could get here by myself then I think, Miss Nora, that you can also find the way back to your room or any other room you fancy.'

'You really said that? She must have been smarting!'

'If she has the gall to try and steal someone's husband then I'm gutsy enough to say something!'

Wati turned into the parking lot of Lake Gardens.

'We're already here; I didn't realise it,' said Sofia. She stared at the lamps on the surface of the water which was calm without any ripples. She recalled one time when she and Halim were fishing in the lake at the back of their house. Those were sweet memories ... sweet memories which she would not let go. The sweet memories gave rise to feelings of utter sorrow. What was the use of remembering something that caused sadness.

'You're still brooding,' said Wati. 'We can have satay or laksa or noodles at the stall by the lake there. After that we can go anywhere you like. My husband is in Kaloi. I can sleep over at your place tonight, if you want.'

'Rahim is here,' said Rokiah. 'Poor Rahim, when he comes, Wati is never here.' She turned toward Malisa who was about to take a mouthful of rice.

Malisa stopped in her tracks and washed her hands. Perhaps Rahim would want to dine together. Rice needed to be cooked. She rushed to the kitchen and was in the middle of washing the rice when Rahim came in holding some fruit. She didn't look up but could feel him standing next to her.

'Can I wash my hands?' whispered Rahim.

Malisa did not turn. She tried to stop her heart from pounding. She pulled the rice pot to the side allowing Rahim to wash his hands.

'Why are your hands dirty?' asked Malisa moving away to place the rice pot on the stove.

'I had a flat tyre on the way.'

'Is everything all alright?'

'Everything's fine. I just had to put on a new tyre.'

'Rahim, do you want some paraffin? If you rub your hands it with paraffin, the black oil will disappear,' said Malisa taking out some paraffin from the cupboard.

Rahim was still washing his hands at the tap. Malisa brought the bottle of paraffin over to him. Rahim opened both his hands and Malisa poured the fluid slowly onto them.

'More,' said Rahim.

'Is this enough for you?'

'I meant a lot, not a little.'

Malisa smiled, then she saw a cut on Rahim's arm.

'What's wrong with your arm, Rahim? There's blood!

A cut like this needs antiseptic, if not it could get infected.'

'It's nothing,' said Rahim, as he rubbed the oil stains off his hands.

'Rokiah! Do you have any antiseptic?' called Malisa. Rokiah was in the bathroom.

'In the cupboard!' answered Rokiah.

Malisa returned with a bottle of antiseptic, bandage and cotton.

'Hey that stings!' said Rahim. 'Please don't.'

'You're like a child, afraid of medicine,' said Malisa putting the bottle of antiseptic and cloth on the kitchen table. She held out a towel for Rahim to wipe his hands.

'Are the stains gone?'

'Yes, all gone.'

Malisa moved nearer to Rahim. She took the towel from his hand and placed it on the table. The cut on the arm was quite large.

'What happened?' asked Malisa as she held Rahim's arm.

'I don't know, I didn't realise it had happened.'

'Eh, stay still. I want to apply the antiseptic.' She held Rahim's arm tightly this time and poured the antiseptic on to the cut. He jumped and hollered in pain.

Malisa shook her head and began bandaging the cut with the white cloth.

'Why don't you just put on a plaster?' she heard Rokiah say from behind.

'Ah, no need. The bandage is better. Air can come in and it will dry and heal faster.'

'Alright, madam doctor!'

'You're always teasing!' said Malisa.

'Eh, what's that smell?' asked Rokiah.

Rahim began to sniff the air.

'The rice is burnt!' screamed Malisa. 'I forgot it was cooking on the stove!'

Malisa grabbed the black pot and thrust it under the tap. The rice was ruined.

'Let's go and buy some rice at the junction over there,' said Rahim, 'Lisa, do you have a container?'

She handed it to him but he shook his head. 'Eh, Lisa you must come along, if there's no parking, I can wait in the car.'

'O.K.,' said Malisa.

'Lisa don't get anything for me. I've already eaten and tonight, I've a class,' said Rokiah.

'If so, there's no need to bring this container,' said Rahim as he put it down on the table. 'We'll just eat there.'

Malisa was already outside and did not hear what Rahim said. She slipped into her rubber sandals and opened the gates.

Rahim started the car. When he arrived at the gates, Rahim said: 'Leave the gates open, Rokiah is going out later.'

Malisa opened the door of the Mercedes and climbed in.

'Eh, I forgot, tonight she has English class. Thank God I brought the house key, if not we wouldn't have been able to get back into the house.'

Rahim smiled meaningfully as he turned toward Malisa on his left. He'd suddenly realized that he'd left behind the key that Wati had given him. What would they have done if Lisa really had forgotten to bring her house key? He shook his head and tried to stop speculating. Sometimes human beings could not control their thoughts. Curiosity sometimes led their thoughts down unhelpful paths.

As soon as they arrived at Seroja Road, they could see many cars parked at the roadside. Fortunately, there was a car reversing to go out. Rahim hurriedly drove his Mercedes into the vacant space.

'Where's the food container?' asked Malisa as she opened the car door.

'I left it behind!' said Rahim.

'Why?'

'Eh, we should just eat here, it's easier and there's no need to do the dishes.'

'You and your excuses,' said Malisa. She closed the door on her side again.

Rahim opened the door on the driver side. 'Eh, how's this, you close and I open!'

'I'm not eating here. Look at those people there, all nicely dressed. I'm in my scruffy outfit and sandals. You go ahead.'

'Oh come on, your outfit isn't scruffy, it's attractive,' said Rahim as he stepped out of the car. He went to the door on Malisa's side, and opened the door. Malisa showed a long face, indicating refusal.

'Try smiling a little!' Rahim gazed at Malisa. Malisa smiled. 'Ha! There, I can see your sweet dimples ... not dirty at all!'

'Ala ... it feels embarrassing with these sandals!'

'It was okay if you had to go and buy the food?'

'If I buy the food and put it into the container it's alright. But I feel embarrassed to eat here!'

Rahim grabbed Malisa's hand, trying to pull her out of the car. 'Come on, we're already here. People are looking,'

He was still holding Malisa's hand. Malisa's heart was pounding. When she was a little girl, she once held hands with Ali as they were running away, chased by geese. But she had never felt her heart beat this way. Malisa tried not to look at Rahim. She pulled her hand away slowly.

'If you don't want to get down, I'll bring the food here. What would you like?' asked Rahim.

'Stewed noodles and peanut ice,' said Malisa.

Rahim moved away from there.

Malisa closed her eyes. Oh God, what is happening to me? She tried to calm herself but she could still feel Rahim's breath when he was washing his hands earlier. They had never been that close before. And just now, he had held my hand, asking me to get out of the car.

Malisa closed her mouth with her left hand with the hope that her train of thoughts would stop but she could not help it. She could not stop her mind from thinking. She had never felt this way before.

A while later Rahim returned with a small boy. Malisa opened the door on her side. Rahim held out a bowl of stewed noodles to her. He returned to the door on the driver side. He opened the door and took a plate of fried noodles from the boy.

'Put the rest on the back seat,' he told the boy and then turned to Malisa. 'I also ordered peanut ice, it looked too delicious to resist!'

Malisa was still silent.

The boy closed the back door and left.

'Hey, you're not eating,' Rahim said.

Malisa turned to Rahim. She smiled.

'Still hot,' said Malisa. 'You go ahead and eat your noodles. It'll get cold.'

Rahim tasted the noodles a little.'Hey, this is great. No wonder you like to buy food at this junction.'

'Yes, the food here is delicious,' said Malisa, as she mixed the steamed noodles with her spoon, but was afraid to bring

134

them to her mouth, because they were still too hot.

Rahim looked at her. 'Eh, what are you staring at? Don't think too much, or you'll be destroyed,' said Rahim. 'Here, try this! The spoon filled with noodles was brought near Malisa's lips.

'You don't have to,' said Malisa.

She began to have some of her stewed noodles. But she still did not want to talk a lot. Rahim became concerned. 'Lisa, are you worried about going out with me? Are you afraid your boyfriend might be angry?'

'*Ala* ... Rahim, I don't have any boyfriends.'

'Don't try to hide it! I know you have a lot of admirers.'

'There's no one. It's true. Why would I lie?' Lisa tried to eat the stewed noodles. They were her favourite but now they just tasted bland. '*Ala*, I don't know how to dress up, how to do my hair and make up. I'm just an ordinary girl!'

'Eh, if the face is already pretty, the smile already sweet with dimples, there's no need to be stylish or made up,' Said Rahim. 'Those with powder and lipstick are the ones who have something to conceal, a pimple or wrinkled cheeks to hide. But Lisa is just attractive this way.'

Malisa turned to her right and found that Rahim was still gazing at her. She stared at Rahim's face - something she never tired of doing. Rahim's eyes felt sharp, piercing Malisa's heart. Her whole body felt weak when Rahim looked at her that way. Malisa would not give in to impossible feelings. No, she would not give in.

Rahim took the bowl of noodles from Malisa's lap.'Why are you not eating?'

'I've had enough ... I don't want to eat anymore.'

Rahim sipped the sauce with a spoon.

Malisa glanced from the corner of her eyes but did not dare to say anything.

'You're too quiet tonight,' said Rahim. 'There must be something bothering you.'

Malisa was still silent.

Rahim put his plate and bowl in the tray in the back seat. He reached for the two glasses of special shaved ice with garnishings and passed one to Malisa. 'I'm afraid the shaved ice has melted.'

'Ah it doesn't matter.'

'Lisa , why is it I have an odd feeling that you don't want to talk to me this evening?'

Malisa turned to Rahim. Her hair covered part of her wide forehead. Rahim was puzzled at the way Malisa was looking at him. Looking without smiling, thought Rahim.

'I don't know, Rahim, my heart suddenly feels melancholy.'

'Perhaps you're thinking about your hometown?'

'Perhaps!'

'Tomorrow I'm going back to Kaloi. If you want, you can come with me. I pass by Kampung Serindik on the way to Kaloi.'

'Hmm, I'll think about it...' she said.

'Lisa, if you're sad, I feel troubled too. Whenever I come, you're always cheerful, but today you're so gloomy...'

'Let's go back,' said Malisa.

'Finish up your shaved ice.'

'Oh, I just can't.'

'O.K., let's go then.'

The Wife

'Wati, if you're weren't with me right now, I don't know what would happen.' Sofia put her head down on the blue pillow case. She didn't want to sleep in her room.

'Be patient Sofia, don't give up. Whatever happens, don't let Halim go. Why should we so easily hand over our husbands to cheap women? Because we're always giving in, that's why it's so easy for them to win.'

Wati put on Sofia's blouse and Javanese sarong. She would spend the night there to keep her best friend company. Wati was worried about leaving Sofia on her own and in any case tomorrow was Sunday. It was not a working day.

Sofia tried to close her eyes but her mind was in a mess.

'You know something?' she said as she turned toward Wati, who was about to lie down on the other bed. 'When you told me that story about how Halim brought all three of his girlfriends to the dance, I didn't want to believe it, but after he brought both of us on a honeymoon to Tokyo, I now understand that he would indeed do such a thing.'

'You didn't believe me when I told you about it?'

'It wasn't that I didn't believe you, but it was just difficult to accept the whole thing. Now I understand! Now, I will no longer trust Halim. No more!'

'Don't give up, Sofia. We're still young; the world is big,' said Wati.

'If you were me, would you find another man?'

'If I were you, it would not even bother me.'

'Yes, you can find other guys, because you need not depend on Rahim. You have your own money, you can take care of yourself, you would not be left begging, but my situation is different. I cannot go anywhere. My mother in the village depends on my brother who is farming. I don't want to be a burden to them. He already has many children. If Halim wants to leave me, I am in God's hands. I couldn't go back to my hometown. But I must trust that God is always on my side no matter what happens.'

'Halim will not leave you. He loves you wholeheartedly,' said Wati, trying to pacify her.

'While he loves me wholeheartedly, he still had the nerve to bring Nora along to Tokyo. Imagine if he didn't love me, Imagine what his actions would be then.'

'Ah, don't think of such stuff. Try to get some sleep. You surely haven't had enough sleep.'

'Yes, I haven't slept since that night,' said Sofia. 'You go ahead and sleep. I'll sleep later....'

Sofia tried to close her eyes, but was unable to sleep. She thought about her children who were far away. When she thought about them, she steeled herself to go through life with an injured heart.

Malisa woke up. Her dreams had been disturbed by a disturbing sound. She rubbed her eyes and looked at the clock next to the table, which indicated that it was two o'clock in the morning. She wondered what it was that she had heard. Malisa got up and went to her door and listened. The sound was getting louder.

Ah, the television set! They had forgotton to switch it off.

Malisa silenced it and went to the kitchen for some water. She poured a glass and took it over to the middle of the house.

In the darkness, Malisa could see someone sleeping on the long couch. All the lights had been switched off. She knew Rokiah often slept there after watching a movie so she put the glass on the table and approached the couch.

'Rokiah ... wake up ... you should go to bed...' said Malisa. She moved even closer.

Rahim felt someone touching his shoulder. He was half awake. Perhaps he was in a dream. He felt someone sitting near him. Rahim held out his hand and grasped Malisa's waist.

'You just got home, Wati? What time is it now? You just got back?' His eyes were still shut and he thought that it was Wati who was sitting next to him.

It was only then Malisa realised that this was Rahim sleeping on the couch and not Rokiah. The hand that was on what she thought was Rokiah's shoulder was lifted immediately. But she felt Rahim's hand still around her waist.

'Rahim!' The word blurted out of Malisa's mouth. 'I'm sorry, I thought it was Rokiah sleeping here.' She tried to get away from Rahim's embrace, but he just gripped her tighter.

Rahim opened his eyes slowly. In the dim of the night he saw Malisa, not Wati. Slowly, his hand released Malisa. The girl's heart was pounding. She was shocked. As she got up, her hand was grabbed by Rahim.

'Wait Malisa ... wait,' whispered Rahim.

Malisa froze. Only her heart was moving. Her entire body felt weak.

Rahim sat up on the couch. Slowly, he pulled Malisa down eside him.

'What's wrong?' Malisa's voice was hesitant.

'Sit down for a while!' whispered Rahim.

Malisa sat close to Rahim. Too close, she felt. Much too close.

'I had a terrible nightmare. I can feel it even now,' he held Malisa's hand even tighter. 'You know those nightmares, the ones that feel so real...'

Malisa turned toward Rahim. She felt she could hear Rahim's heartbeat. In the dark, she looked at Rahim's face and saw that he was sweating.

'What was the dream about?' asked Malisa. She allowed Rahim to hold her hand.

'I dreamed of Wati. I dreamed she was running into the jungle. I felt terrified thinking about the jungle, filled with thorns and undergrowth. I ran after her.' He clasped Malisa's hand tightly. 'I ran for miles. I was sweating, Malisa. I feel the tiredness even now.'

Malisa looked at Rahim's face. Her left hand had been in Rahim's hand all the time. Malisa touched Rahim's sweaty forehead.

'Would you like some water?' Malisa reached for the glass of water she had taken earlier. She handed it over to Rahim and he drank. He placed the glass back onto the table.

'Let me get some more water,' said Malisa. She stood up and felt Rahim releasing her hand slowly.

Malisa had to move away quickly. She could not bear to be that close to Rahim. She went to the kitchen again, opened the refrigerator and poured some cold water into the glass. She returned to the middle of the house. Rahim was still on the couch.

'What time is it now?'

'Two thirty, I think,' said Malisa, stopping with the glass

in her hand. Her heart was pounding again.

'Is Wati always this late?'

'No! Usually she's home early,' said Malisa. 'She's never been this late. It's best that you sleep inside. There are lots of mosquitoes here.'

She left Rahim and went to her room. She took a sip of her drink and placed the glass on her dresser. She could still feel her heart pounding. Why was she feeling like this when she was with Rahim? Malisa did not want to think about this. She was aware that she was beginning to weaken whenever she was near Rahim. She could still feel Rahim's earlier embrace. She could still feel her hand being tightly held. Oh Rahim! Malisa felt emotional. She threw herself on the bed. She cried her heart out.

In the middle of the house, Rahim was still sitting, transfixed. Where could Wati be this late? I knew she was wild when I married her. But I did not know she would behave like this after marriage. Rahim tried not to think too much. He wondered if she should go out and look for Wati, perhaps she had been involved in a car accident somewhere. But ... surely Wati would have come home by taxi. Wati is used to going out alone. She can look after herself. Rahim tried to calm his thoughts but could not succeed.

10

FROM a distance, Sofia heard a slow sad song, piercing her soul and pressing on her chest. Sofia did not want to hear music like this which only increased her anguish. She didn't want to listen to songs that made her think painfully of past things, her youth, a time of happiness.

I cannot look backwards. I need to face the future even if it is bristling with thorns, even if it is filled with bitter poison.

The happiness of her youth could not possibly heal the suffering she was feeling. In fact, those memories intensified the bitterness in her heart. Sofia kept thinking about the wonderful times she had, especially playing by the small river. After she had gone for Quran reading classes in the afternoons, Sofia loved to walk in the fast-flowing stream. She often found flowers floating around her legs. She knew that the flowers were thrown in the water by Halim who was following her from behind.

Ah forget it ... forget it! I have already told Halim that my love for him is gone. But, that is my love for Halim now, whereas the love for Halim then is still flaming in my heart, she whispered silently. Yes ... that was then, but this is now. Halim is not the same Halim as then. Halim is now someone with a high position, rich and wealthy. Halim was then the son of a farmer.

Then his love was sincere and pure but now love can be bought and sold.

142

The Wife

Perhaps that is why I cannot let go of old memories because they are associated with authentic values, traditional values. Love then was pure. Love now... ah, forget it! Haven't I promised not to look back? Pure love is a myth. No regrets. Is being alone my destiny? I promise I will face the future bravely and patiently. Even with a soul that is void of feeling. Regardless of what happens, I will face it calmly.

The telephone rang. Sofia walked slowly towards it. Slowly she picked it up. 'Hello?'

It was Rahmah. 'Hello, Sofia, are you going to the meeting today?'

'I don't feel well,' Sofia found she was beginning to lie more often. Now she understood why people liked to lie.

'What's wrong? Since you became friends with that Fatimawati, you've dropped me. Always sick or a headache. Can I come over to see you?'

'I can't stop you, can I?'

'Alright, I'll come by after the meeting.'

'Thank you, please send my regards to *datin*,' said Sofia.

'O.K. Goodbye.'

She replaced the telephone.

She heard Halim's car coming into the yard. The door was not locked, refreshments were already waiting on the table. His towel and sarong were ready on the bed.

Sofia went to the kitchen. She could still hear the melancholy music from her neighbour's house. She opened the kitchen door to the backyard, put on her sandals and went down the steps. She started watering her orchids. The beautiful songs were still playing. Softly, faintly....

As Halim closed the car door he noticed that Sofia's car was there. He went inside and straight to his room where his towel and sarong were on the bed. In the afternoon he would be going out to play golf. He ignored the towel and sarong, took his golf shirt and quickly went downstairs.

He approached the dining table. The food cover was lifted, and he saw the sweetmeats, onde-onde, which was his favourite, served with tea.

Halim was in a hurry to play golf and didn't want to eat, so he grabbed his golf clubs beside the stairs and headed for the door. The gates were still open. Sofia wasn't visible, but he heard her in the kitchen and then also heard someone watering the plants. He put on his golf shoes and left.

Halim turned the car out of the drive way. Today he was playing golf with Datuk Kassim, so he must not be late.

Since they got back from Tokyo, Sofia seldom spoke. In a day, they often only exchanged two or three sentences, and only when necessary. They did not talk or joke as they used to.

At first, Halim tried to win back Sofia's heart, but it seemed impossible. Sofia was like someone in a dream world. Her soul was far away. At times, she appeared not to hear what was said to her.

But she was still punctilious about housework. Every evening she prepared sweetmeats, and served tea at the table. Every night dinner was served whether or not Halim came home. But she did not dine with Halim. If Halim asked her to join him, she would simply say that she had eaten.

After Halim had left, Sofia found herself wandering across the yard and out through the open gate.

Halim had tried everything to coax her from her dark place but Sofia remained unmoved. She could not forget

144

her humiliation in Tokyo. Each time she thought about it, it pained her.

Once, her priority was to protect her family, to defend the harmony of her marriage from all kinds of threats. But what about now? She had become weak, she simply let the situation be. She no longer wanted to pour out all her love on this family which she had once cherished. Was there the possibility of happiness without love? What is the point of marriage without love?

No, oh no! Sofia struggled within her heart. When Halim was with his lover he was only thinking about himself. This meant that Halim sought love elsewhere. This meant Halim did not lack for love or caresses.

What is your duty Sofia? What is your duty? She heard again the small voice protesting.

With the way he humiliated me, my duty has ceased to exist. I am no longer the queen in the dream palace, but a slave that prepares food for him, cleans for him, Sofia tried to respond.

Hah! If that is so, then you have torn up your vow. You once promised that you would fight all enemies so that the king in your dream palace will not be harmed. But now, you are encouraging its destruction. You are encouraging him to lose control. You are encouraging him to be wild!

Ah, enough! Enough! Why should I be the one to take responsibility, why? Men are always in the right; even if they commit a crime, the fault is on the wife for letting him do it. If the wife is in control, it is still her fault for being too harsh!

Men are indeed not to be blamed. And that is just because they are men. Sofia could feel a headache. She remembered that she had not eaten since morning. The road span before her and she fell down unconscious.

She tried to open her eyes but could not.

'Hang on, madam, you fainted.' Someone was saying.

'Where am I?' asked Sofia, holding out her hand. Someone took it slowly. She felt it held tight.

'Madam, don't worry, I'm a doctor. There's nothing seriously wrong with you, I think. You're probably not well, perhaps you didn't eat enough today, perhaps you're over-tired.'

The doctor's face was blurred when Sofia opened her eyes. He touched her forehead with the back of his hand.

Sofia tried to get up.

'Where am I?' Sofia was looking at a man in shorts and a T-shirt.

Halim did not know what else to do. He had tried everything to improve Sofia's mood, but she remained cold, detached. She no longer went out and mixed with people like she used to. She preferred to be alone with her orchids.

Hmm, I really do not know, thought Halim. I do not understand that woman. What does she really want? I have given her everything. A house, a car, jewellery, nice clothes. Is that not enough?

It's not that I haven't tried. It's not that I haven't apologised. I have done so, many times. Does she want me to beg?

Human beings have their limits. I am tired of pleading with her every day. It is up to her whether she wants to talk or not. If I say anything, it might be the wrong thing, if I do not say anything, it might also be wrong.

'You fainted in front of my house and I brought you inside,' said the man. 'My name is Subardi.'

'Thank you, forgive me; I'm troubling you, sir.'

'Just call me Subardi,' said Dr. Subardi smiling. 'Drink some milk and you may feel better.'

'I'm Sofia.' She reached for the milk.

'Sofia ... in Indonesia, I had a friend named Sofia. I've not seen her for a long time. I don't know where she's now!'

'Not this one. I've never been to Indonesia!'

'Oh! Oh! Yes I know ... not this one because the Sofia I know has a mole on her right cheek.'

'If you met her, would you recognise her?' asked Sofia. She drank some more of the milk.

'Maybe, maybe I would recognise her. But we haven't met for a really long time. She probably has grown-up children.'

'She must be rather special,' Sofia smiled placing the cup on the table.

'Ah ... an old story. She probably doesn't remember me.'

Sofia got up. Her headache was slowly fading. 'I must go. Thank you for your kindness.'

Dr. Subardi nodded. Smiling, he stroked his thin moustache with the back of his fore finger.

'Thank you, see you again,' said Sofia, smiling.

Dr. Subardi accompanied Sofia to the gate. Sofia noticed the number 1912, on the wall. She stopped.

'Subardi!' She turned toward him, her right hand covering her mouth as if in surprise.

Dr. Subardi was still looking at her.

'Are you the one who's been playing those songs on the organ?' Sofia asked.

Dr. Subardi smiled. 'Forgive me if those songs disturb you, madam.'

'Sofia ... call me Sofia.'

'Yes, forgive me if....'

'Eh no ... I really like those songs.'

'They're old songs.'

'Yes, I loved those songs when I was younger. A long time ago!'

'Hey, Sofia, you're not as old as that! Please! Don't make me laugh.'

Sofia smiled.

'Walk carefully. Or would you like me to drive you home?'

'No it's near. Over there.' Sofia pointed toward her house.

'I know where you live.'

'You know?'

'Yes, you always walk in front of this house.'

'Oh!'

'We'll see each other again.'

'Thank you.' Sofia left the place, the white house number 1912, Selasih Road.

The Wife

'Come on! Eat up! Is everyone watching their figure?' said Zaharah.

'Huh ... no point in taking care of this body ... still like a barrel,' said Madam Kalsom.

'Isn't Sofia coming, Rahmah?' asked Halimah.

'I telephoned her earlier ... she said she was not well,' answered Rahmah. 'She sends her best regards to you.'

'What's wrong with her? These two, three months she has been keeping to herself. If there are meetings, she never comes,' said Datin Zaharah.

Rahmah was silent. She didn't want to say anything.

'Rahmah, don't you have any news?' said Kalsom.

'What news?' asked Rahmah.

'Well, you're her good friend ... as if you don't know? Everyone knows, how is it that her good friend doesn't know?'

'I haven't met her in a while,' said Rahmah. 'My mother is ill, in the village, so I had to go back.'

'Hmm, taking care of your mother in the village ... if we're not careful our husbands would be snatched by others!' said Kalsom.

Everyone laughed.

'Eh not your husband, Rahmah! We're just reminding everyone,' said Halimah.

'I don't understand!' said Rahmah.

'Well, tell her a little bit ... poor girl, she doesn't know anything!' said Shamsiah.

'Don't talk about others, that's gossiping.'

'We're not gossiping, we're talking about this situation as

149

an example so that we all can learn from it. If we don't stay alert then our husbands will make fools of us and we'll all be left like Sofia!' said Kalsom.

It hurt Rahmah to hear that. She didn't like people to criticize others, particularly her own good friend. She felt rather angry.

'Well, Rahmah is pretending not to know,' said Shamsiah.

'No, I really have no idea. Sofia never talks about her private life.'

'Rahmah, after this we all have to be more careful now. If you go back too long to take care of your ailing mother, who'll take care of your husband?' said Datin Zaharah.

They all laughed, but Rahimah was still confused.

'Look at Rahmah, poor thing, she genuinely doesn't know what we're laughing about,' said Kalsom. 'Listen, Rahmah, recently, we heard a story and I'm sorry to say that it's about Sofia. But we're not gossiping about her, remember, we only want it to be a reminder.'

'If so, tell me, what's there to be afraid of,' Said Rahmah.

'Recently, her husband took her on a work trip to Tokyo,' said Kalsom.

'What's wrong with that?' asked Rahmah. She was beginning to get angry with the sneers.

'Of course there's nothing wrong with going to Tokyo,' added Kalsom. 'But what really happened?'

'What happened?' asked Rahmah.

'Who could ever imagine it!' Shamsiah interrupted.

'Indeed, men cannot be trusted! Oh ... it makes me really upset!' said Kalsom.

'What happened?' asked Rahmah again.

'Sofia didn't know, but her husband also brought another

woman along!' said Kalsom.

'I don't believe it!' said Rahmah. 'I really don't believe it. Halim's a good man, he's very courteous.'

'You think he's a good man! I suppose if you see him, he looks like an ideal husband, but if he had brought along his mistress together with his wife on their honeymoon, I wouldn't say that he's a good man anymore,' said Datin Zaharah.

'Yes, datin, if my husband behaved like an animal, I would strangle him!' said Shamsiah.

'We would have a criminal case then!' said Kalsom.

They all laughed again.

Rahmah could not contain her anger anymore. Her heart was beating faster. Perhaps this was why Sofia did not want to come and was gloomy these days. But surely not. Sure this couldn't be true...

'I don't believe it,' she said. 'How do you all know about it?'

'Do you know that Sofia came back earlier than Halim and that woman?'

'Is that right Kalsom?'

'Yes, Mr Rahman saw her returning, crying and hugging Fatimawati at the airport,' said Kalsom further.

'If she came back alone, that means they came back later then,' said Shamsiah.

'Oh if that's so, she gave him the opportunity!' said Halimah.

'Huh ... if it were me, I wouldn't have come home alone. That means defeat. I wouldn't give my husband so easily to another woman, particularly one who's as cheap as that,' said Shamsiah.

'If it were you, what would you do, Shamsiah?' asked

Datin Zaharah.

'If it were me, I would beat the hell out of that woman in front of my husband. Let him see it for himself. I would like to see what he would do.'

'Sham, if the husband takes our side, that would be alright. If he goes to the other woman's side, and holds her, afraid that we might beat him next, wouldn't you be furious?' said Kalsom.

'If my husband did that, I would hit him too,' said Shamsiah further. 'Well by then I wouldn't be ashamed of anything, I would ... be really furious!'

Rahmah got up because she could not bear listening to their conversation anymore.'My kid has extra class today. I must go and pick her up. Excuse me, alright.' She shook hands with Datin Zaharah and everyone there.

'Remember this Saturday there's a religious talk at the mosque. Everyone must attend. I must show people that I'm very firm in my religion,' said Datin Zaharah. 'Don't forget to bring your scarf....'

'Should we be all covered *datin*?' asked Halimah.

'You must be covered. How can you go to the mosque without being covered?' said Shamsiah before Datin Zaharah could answer.

'Alright *datin*,' said Rahmah. '*In-sha-Allah*, if there's no obstacles, I'll come.'

'Don't say *in-sha-Allah*, you must come,' said Kalsom.

'Yes, *in-sha-Allah*,' said Rahmah. Perhaps Kalsom did not understand the meaning of *in-sha-Allah*, she thought.

Rahmah left the place feeling extremely sad. She felt sympathy for Sofia, who did not know that people were talking behind her back. In front of her, they would be talking about something else.

At first, I assumed they were sincere, but I am no longer certain, thought Rahmah. I need to go to Sofia's house to learn the truth. I do not want them to slander her behind her back. She must go to the next meeting to explain everything.

'Are you going home right away?' asked Wati. This time she was wearing a pair of tight, white pants, with a green and purple striped long sleeved shirt.

'Ah, it doesn't matter if I don't go home!' said Halim adjusting his cap.

They headed towards the golf club. Two caddies were following them as they pulled the trolley of golf clubs.

'Would you like to have a drink first at the golf club?' asked Wati.

'Hmm, alright ... where else can I go?'

'The way you talk, it's as if you don't have a family, no wife. If I speak like that, it's alright. My husband is far away, my house is only like a hotel,'

'Wati, since I came back from Tokyo, Sofia has become like a robot. If I say something, she moves. If not, she would still there aimlessly.'

'You speak as though you're bored.'

'You would be bored too. Imagine if every time you went home there was nothing but silence; no laughter, no jokes; wouldn't you be bored?'

'Isn't that your fault? I reminded you long ago, but you refused to listen. You think that you can behave like when

153

you were in the university, bringing three dates to a dance?'

Halim stopped walking andWati also stopped, puzzled.

'Eh, how did you know?' asked Halim as he held Wati's arm.

'Ala ... whatever you do I know, understand?' Wati smiled. Halim released her hand. They continued walking.

'I don't believe you!' said Halim, turning to Wati. She gave him a meaningful smile again.

'You don't believe it?'

'No. Whatever you do, I know too!' said Halim.

'Ah ... I haven't done anything,'

'I don't believe it!'

Both of them laughed and then they arrived at the golf club. Halim immediately ordered a drink and sat close to Wati. Wati took off her sunglasses, cupping her chin with her two palms.

Halim took a chair at the round table facing Wati. His knee almost touched Wati's. He stared at Wati's face.

'Hey Wati ... if you put on your black sunglasses, you look more like your cousin who likes to eat peanuts in the garden over there!' Halim laughed.

'You're a tease.' Wati pinched Halim's arm.

'It's true. Around your eyes, you're white and the rest is dark!' said Halim, laughing again and moving nearer to Wati, his knees touching Wati's knees.

Wati laughed but moved backwards, so that she could not feel Halim's knees.

They took the drinks brought over by a young Chinese man.

'How's Sofia? I haven't seen her in a while. As you know, I've only just got back from Sabah.'

The Wife

'Sofia ... Sofia ... I don't know! I don't want to think about it. I don't know what else to say to her.'

'She surely has forgiven you!'

'Yes, she says she has, but she's not like before. She used to be loving. She was the ideal wife for me, never protesting, never putting on a sour face. Now....'

'She's hurt, Halim. If your heart is bitterly hurt, you wouldn't want to laugh. Our face shows our feelings. If we're sad, we cannot appear happy,' said Wati.

'I still don't understand. I'm not as bad as I used to be. I come home early. I don't go out at night. I'm a good man. At night I sit home and watch TV.'

'Oh really?' Wati mocked, blinking her eyes.

'It's true. You don't believe me? Come and see for yourself.'

'I'm busy now with Datuk Kassim's proposal. He has a seminar in Colombo soon.'

'You're not going along?'

'No, I'm a bit busy.'

'Busy with what?'

'After I finish his proposal, I have to prepare your proposal,' said Wati.

'Which one then?'

'You need to go to Indonesia at the end of July.'

'Well, I don't know anything about that,' said Halim puzzled.

'Well, what do you know ... you're only basking in the glory. The ones who do the work are us.'

'Hey, don't say that. If you want to go abroad, you can do so anytime.'

'Datuk did ask me to go along to Indonesia, but I refused. I go there all the timea anyway, so I'll give the chance to others like you. Plus I'm a woman: going there would be a waste of time,' said Wati, smiling cynically.

Halim was about to open his mouth to defend himself from the snide remark, but no words came out.

'What happened to that Nora?' asked Wati.

'I don't know.' Halim wanted to avoid the topic.

'You should try to control her a bit! She seems a bit obsessive. If you take the wrong step, you'll be in danger!'

'What do you mean?'

'I know women like ther. If she wants you, she'll not stop half way. She'll do anything.'

'Don't try to scare me, Wati.' Halim was beginning to feel frightened.

'You should know that once a woman becomes angry, she can do anything. If she's not strong in her faith, she might consult a shaman. She can stupefy you!' said Wati, 'and if you become stupefied, you'll forget your work and everything else.'

'Is that true Wati?'

'I'm not winding you up. I'm telling the truth. If you don't believe me, ask anyone. I don't dare to cross people who are so worldly.'

'I have to find a spiritual guru then!'

'Even if you had a spiritual gutu, what could they do if you continued to be too intimate with that girl?' said Wati. 'The guru should be within yourself. If you can control your lust, that's your guru, if you cannot, ha, you'll become that girl's victim.'

'How is it that you know everything, Wati? Spiritual knowledge, witchcraft. You've got a spiritual guru, perhaps? Or perhaps you've used black magic yourself, that's why your husband's tame, not wild like other men. You must have done something to him. If it were me, my wife leaving me alone like that, why would I stay home and wait? And even if I stayed home every night, that could be just as dangerous!'

'Why?'

'There would be a party!' said Halim.

'You're rambling. If Rahim had such a party in Kampung Kaloi, ha, the next day he would be jobless,' said Wati. They laughed and Wati got up, along with Halim. Both of them left.

11

'**AMINAH**, is Mr Halim here yet?' asked Rogayah as she took her seat.

'Not yet. He has a meeting at 9.00 in the operations room. He might go there directly,' said Aminah.

'Have you heard the latest news?'

'What news?'

'The other day, while you were out for a while, she came in crying.'

'Hmm, what happened?' Aminah was curious.

'I don't know much really but according to our mole, her boss was furious. He's tired of her antics. She's been transferred to another place,' said Rogayah.

'Still in this building?'

'Ah, surely not ... to another building.'

'Well something must be wrong.' Aminah smiled meaningfully to Rogayah.

They both laughed.

'Hey, hey! Talking about others, is that right?' Ahmad poked his head around the door in before coming in, 'I heard. You called me a mole!'

'Ahmad, Ahmad!' Rogayah was shaking her head and giggling. 'What am I going to do about you?'

All of them laughed.

'So... Don't you know the other story?' said Ahmad.

'What story?'

158

'Ah... so you don't know!'

'Regarding what?'

'Eh, what else? Regarding the earlier matter.'

Rogayah looked at Aminah. Aminah did not understand.

'Eh, just tell us!' said Rogayah.

'What treat will I get?' said Ahmad.

'Shaved ice with peanuts?'

'Huh ... not that!'

'Stewed noodles?' asked Aminah.

Just as Ahmad was about to open his mouth, they saw Fatimawati coming in.

'Ahmad! Come to my office.' Wati went into her office.

'Brief disturbance. Don't adjust your television!' said Ahmad, grinning, then left.

'Eh, I wonder what the story is!' said Aminah, curiously.

'Well, what else, it must be about Nora! What else could it be?' said Rogayah.

Ahmad entered Wati's office. Wati had on a black midi skirt and an ocean blue blouse. Her hair was tied to one side.

'Ahmad, what's all that noise about outside?' asked Wati.

Ahmad moved forward, facing Fatimawati. 'Sit down!' said Wati.

Ahmad obeyed.

'What was that all about?' Wati asked seriously.

'It was nothing, madam. We were just joking around.'

'Ahmad, you'd better tell me. Don't lie. I don't like it.'

'Yes, madam!' said Ahmad, looking down.

'About Nora, right?' Wati was setting a trap.

'Yes, madam,' Ahmad said.

'What's happened? I hear that she has been transferred to another place.'

'Yes, madam, but she still goes to Mr Halim's flat near here!' said Ahmad.

'I know Mr Halim's house. It's on Selasih Road,' said Wati.

'But you don't know, madam. Mr Halim is also renting a flat near here. If he wants to rest, he goes there. I've also gone there, madam; sometimes he asks me to bring a file over.'

'Eh, this is really strange!' said Wati but she stopped when she realised that she was speaking to the office boy. 'Do you know the address?'

'Yes, madam.'

'Write the address here,' said Wati and she held out a piece of paper and a pencil.

Ahmad wrote it down.

'If I know this address, it'll be easier for me to find Mr Halim, if we have any problems,' said Wati.

'Yes, madam.'

'Do you see Nora going there?'

'Yes madam, she always goes there.'

'How do you know?'

'I always pass by there on my way back. I often see her there,' said Ahmad.

'Alright, Ahmad. If you haven't told Aminah and Rogayah, don't tell them, otherwise they'd tell everyone that you like to spread rumours. If they tell Mr Halim, you will be transferred from here. Remember that!'

'Yes, madam, I won't tell them. I hope you'll not tell Mr Halim that I told you.' Ahmad was beginning to worry.

Ahmad left Wati deep in thought. It appeared that Halim still had a relationship with Nora. He said he watched TV at home at night. He wanted to convince Sofia that he had changed, but at midday he was at the flat. Ahmad would not

160

lie. What would he get for lying like that?

Ah let them be! Isn't that his business, why should I care? Would I have the heart to tell Sofia? Sofia is now like a ghost, without a soul or feelings. She answers a question with only two or three words. She is living in her own world, her own lonely world.

Now Sofia perceives that her husband is tamed because he comes home every night and he does not go out every night as he used to. But she doesn't know that he spends his lunch breaks resting at his secret flat.

What should I do? I regret calling Ahmad in earlier. I regret forcing Ahmad to tell me about Nora. If I didn't know then I wouldn't have to worry over it. If Rahim was misbehaving, I would like to know, I would like to be informed, I would want to take action, good or bad. This is happening to Sofia and I have to tell her. But I don't know what will happen when Sofia knows. She's already lost hope. If she finds about the flat then who can tell what might happen.

So I cannot speak to Sofia. But I must help in some way. I must help her because she is my friend.

But what can I do?

Sofia had got a new recipe from a magazine. Each time Sofia got a new recipe, she had to try it out. Rahmah often wondered why Sofia cooked relentlessly when Halim seldom ate at home. Cooking had always been one of Sofia's favourite pastimes. Halim used to love her cooking, even when she made only simple dishes. But now even if Sofia cooked steak, Halim would not appreciate it. Sofia realised that Halim was not as he used to be. Now Halim interacted more with people, he involved himself more with society. His dressing and eating habits had also changed, following new trends. She could still remember how happy they were when they used to enjoy rice noodles by the river near the junction to her village.

But that was then. At that time, she was happy even if they were only walking hand-in-hand by the river, feeling the softness of the sand that sank with each step. But now, would she need to travel to Tokyo to seek happiness with her own husband?

Thinking about Tokyo, she remembered Nora. Sofia threw the magazine in her hand onto the table. She felt a sudden fury.

The telephone rang. Who would be calling her so early in the morning? Halim had long since gone to the office. Perhaps the call was for him. Perhaps he had not arrived at the office yet. The telephone rang again. Sofia reached for it.

'Hello,' said Sofia.

'Hello Sofia, this is Wati. How're you?'

'I'm fine.'

'What're you doing there, Sofia?'

'Nothing much.'

'When can we go out again? I thought of going to the hair salon.'

'I just washed my hair,' said Sofia, trying to avoid her. She was too lazy to go anywhere.

'How about a facial?'

'Ah, no need for that, thank you. Some other time, alright?'

'I bought a gift for you from Sabah. I'll send it through Halim,' said Wati.

'Why do you have to trouble yourself?' said Sofia.

'No ... no trouble at all,' said Wati. 'Alright, Sofia, if you don't want to go out today, some other day, alright?'

'O.K.'

Wati put down the telephone. She knew that Sofia was avoiding her because she only wanted to be alone. Wati had tried a few times to take her out of herself, but failed.

Wati understood Sofia's feelings. She understood how disappointed Sofia was at having been treated that way by her own husband. Perhaps Sofia's reaction was different than Wati's would have been in similar circumstances. But she could sense the disappointment and suffering Sofia was feeling.

Oh, Sofia ... I am not able and do not know how to help her. If she does not want to release all that is inside her, she will struggle with her problems alone. She will feel lonely in this huge world.

Wati gave a long sigh.

She heard the telephone ringing twice. Wati picked it up.

'Hello! Yes! Yes! Oh, I almost forgot, what time will the meeting start, yes, alright, I'll come now,' said Wati. She got up, hastily reaching for the file in front of her.

There was a car honking outside. Sofia quickly went to the door. She recognised it as Rahmah's car. She had not seen Rahmah for quite a while. Everyone was busy with their own thing.

She opened the door. Rahmah was getting out of the car,

pressing her bag under her armpit.

'Well! It's been a while since I last saw you!' she called.

'Please come in, Rahmah. I hear that your mother isn't well. Is she alright?' asked Sofia.

'*Alhamduli'llah*, a little better.'

They shook hands at the door.

'Come in,' said Sofia.

They sat on the long couch. Rahmah studied her friend and frowned. 'You've become really thin, Sofia. Have you been exercising?'

'I haven't been feeling well these past few days. The other day I fainted in front of Dr. Subardi's house. I was unconscious, you know!' said Sofia.

'Oh! I know Dr. Subardi. He always comes to my house. He and my husband play golf together.'

'I didn't know you knew him,' said Sofia. 'That was the first time I met him even though we live nearby.'

'Poor him. Recently his wife went back to Sumatra; till now she hasn't returned. I wonder what has happened to her.'

'No wonder the other car is no longer there.'

'That one was sold long ago,' said Rahmah. 'Hmm, I don't know. Sometimes I feel afraid thinking about life. It's like floating on a raft on a fast river ... You don't know what's ahead, a rock, piece of wood, waterfall.' Sofia was quiet, trying not to think about her own problems.

'Anyway, the other day, everyone was upset because I had been away too long taking care of my mother. They said to be careful, if we're too busy looking after our mothers, our husbands will be taken care of by another,' said Rahmah.

Sofia was still quiet. Rahmah decided to be frank.

'You know, I, if I don't tell you this, I'd feel rather guilty ...'

164

The Wife

'Tell me what?' asked Sofia, her heart pounding.

'Hmm, I was quite angry hearing what they said. Forever gossiping about other people.'

'What did they say?'

'I wanted to come over right after the meeting, but you weren't in. I was already here, the gates were opened, your house door was not locked, but you weren't home. That's dangerous Sofia, to leave your house like that. The car was in. I was puzzled as to your whereabouts.'

'That was the day I fainted in front of Dr. Subardi's house. Tell me what happened at the meeting.'

'At first they asked why you didn't come. I said, you weren't well. After that they began talking about Tokyo!' said Rahmah.

Sofia was shocked. She never expected them to know what happened to her in Tokyo. She was angry but what could she say? There was indeed a scandal in Tokyo. Why should she hide it? Sofia suppressed her tears. She steeled herself. This is only a test, whispered her heart.

'Sofia,' said Rahmah, holding Sofia's hand gently. 'Trust me Sofia, whatever happens, I'm on your side. Don't think that you're alone in this. We're friends. We need to help each other.' Sofia was silent, deep in thought. Perhaps what they said was right after all, Rahmah thought.

Tears began to flow slowly down Sofia's soft cheeks. She did not look at Rahmah. She could not bear to picture how humiliating it was when she thought about what happened in Tokyo. She covered her face with her two hands and cried.

'Don't cry, Sofia. Be patient and pray. Remember Allah. He's All Powerful. We're only His creatures but He decide everything,' said Rahmah, embracing Sofia.

'I've been too patient, Rahmah,' said Sofia. 'I've known about my husband's affair. I've met the woman face-to-face. We talked about Halim. I wanted to know if she loved Halim or not. At first I thought I would be able to control the situation. I even told her that I was willing to wait for Halim until he was bored with her. But when I saw Halim being so intimate with her, dancing with her and holding her, my heart was hurt, I was truly crushed. What happened to all our promises of living and dying together? There's no need to speak of death; while still alive, he has had a change of heart.'

'Yes, I know Sofia. We experience a lot of things in this life, the bitter and sweet. I also experienced the same problem once but *alhamduli'llah* only now do I feel a bit of calmness. Nevertheless, the scar is still there,' said Rahmah.

'Rahmah, you went throught the same problem? But your husband is a good man, and pious,' said Sofia wiping her tears with the ends of her fingers.

'Now, *alhamduli'llah* but then, well, when he was younger, he was quite wild. Now, he's retired, bald, money is tight. In the old days, it was a different story, I was simply suffering, Sofia,' said Rahmah, rubbing her chest.

'I never knew!' Sofia was bewildered.

'I was also like you once. Quiet, polite. Whatever my husband said, I just went along with. I never protested. I don't like to see women controlling their husbands. But men, when you're too good, they think that they can do anything to us. They think that whatever they do we'll not be angry because we love them. So what do they do? Well, when he was younger, he was handsome, not bald like now. He was a *Romeo* then.

My mother was always ill. You know, in the village, living

with grandchildren. She didn't want to stay with us. And I of course couldn't bear to see her like that. I took care of her for two to three weeks. What happened was, he turned my house into a hotel. My children weren't home; they'd all gone to study. The house was empty. He took his opportunity.'

'How did you find out?' asked Sofia.

'Sofia, we have experience of life, so we know, I don't have to say more,' said Rahmah.

'Then, what happened?'

'I feel upset if I think about it again, but now *alhamduli'llah* after the prayers of my mother and other family members, everything has come right. One afternoon, I arrived back from the village and found the woman was in my house. My husband introduced her as his second wife. My knees felt weak. I nearly fainted right there. But I steeled myself, I prayed a lot.'

Sofia opened her mouth to say something. Her right hand moved towards her open mouth but stopped half way. No words came out.

'Oh Rahmah!' That was all she could say. 'I never knew!'

'Yes, nobody knew here. It happened when I was staying in Jakarta a long time ago. My husband was working in the embassy there.'

'And then what happened?'

'Oh Sofia, I can't describe how I felt when I was told that he had remarried. But that wasn't all, Sofia, that wasn't all!'

'What else happened?'

'She came and stayed with us, you know!' said Rahmah, tears beginning to flow down her cheeks. 'From that day on, I suffered alone. My relatives were far away, I was on my own there, without anyone to depend on.'

'Oh Rahmah, your story is even sadder...' said Sofia crying, sympathising with the misfortunes of her friend.

'I've never told anyone here, they don't know. Perhaps, Dr. Subardi is the only one who knows.'

'I wonder how you could bear it, Rahmah.'

'You don't know the half of it Sofia, I was treated like a maid, cooking, washing, cleaning the house. They were having a merry time.'

'Why didn't you go back to your parents?'

'Sofia, my mother had told me that no matter what happened I was prohibited from leaving my husband. If I'd gone back to her, she wouldn't have accepted me. If I stayed too long taking care of her while she was ill, she'd scold me, saying my place was with my husband. She was right but if I left then who would take care of her?'

'And then what happened? What happened to that woman?'

'I cried for a long time, Sofia, but when my husband retired, she asked for a divorce.'

'Why?'

'You must understand, Sofia, if you're retired, money is tight, you lose your social position, no more having fun here and there. She liked the high life. She was attractive and stylish. If a husband is old and without money and position, what's the use?' said Rahmah. 'When we moved back here, she didn't come along. My husband had to divorce her.'

'I would never have imagined it.'

'Yes, if you see my husband now, you'd never think that he could do such a thing to me, but now he regrets it. He tries to give me everything that he can, but he knows he can never give me back those years. I went through my young adult life with suffering and tears. Now, I'm already old....'

The Wife

'Eh, you're not old!' said Sofia holding Rahmah's shoulders.

'Yes, but not with the same shape as before. Now he buys me nice clothes, but what's the use? I don't desire all that any more. He doesn't realise that love cannot be bought with money. I always tell him, he need not give me anything, as long as he loves me, that's enough,' said Rahmah.

Sofia felt pressure in her throat. She hugged Rahmah with both arms and sobbed. Rahimah's words had pierced the deepest part of her heart. Yes, Sofia knew she did not need anything. She only needed the undivided love of her husband.

'That's enough Sofia. Don't cry anymore,' said Rahmah.

'Yes.' Sofia looked at Rahmah's face. The tears that were flowing down Rahmah's cheeks were wiped away by her tiny fingers. 'Thank you, Rahmah. Your story has made me understand some things. It's taught me about patience. You have actually gone through things even more devastating than I have,' said Sofia.

'Sofia, don't feel ashamed in society. It's the one who's doing the despicable act who should be ashamed. If you haven't done anything wrong, why should you be ashamed? Take this as a challenge, as a test from Allah of your faith. You need to face it with a heart that is calm.'

'But Rahmah, I don't want to face people who are backstabbing me.'

'That's up to you. If you think you won't get any benefit from your interaction with them, why should you force yourself? This world isn't theirs. If you didn't interact with them, you lose nothing. In fact, your life might be better.'

'What do you mean?'

'Well, when we don't have friends, we also don't have quarrels.'

'I don't know, for now, the problem I'm facing is more important than anything else. The rest is insignificant to me.'

They were both silent for a moment.

'Eh, I haven't served any refreshments!' said Sofia. She was suddenly aware that they had been talking for quite a while without having anything to drink.

'Sofia, no need, I should slim a little. I'm going now. There's fish in the car, it'll go off. I was at the market earlier. I thought I would drop by only a short while. I had no idea it would be this long.' Rahmah got up.

'Why didn't you bring in the fish with you?' asked Sofia.

'I forgot! I'll run along now. Come over to the house. Don't stay home alone all the time, it's no good for you,' said Rahmah.

'Why?'

'If we're alone, a lot of things will come to mind. Sometimes, we can't control our wild thoughts. It's better if we go out. Let our anxiety disappear.'

'Alright Rahmah, I'll try,' Sofia held out her hand. She held Rahmah's hand tightly. 'Thank you so much Rahmah. I'll never forget your kindness.'

'Neither will I forget yours,' said Rahmah.

'Your story has lifted the burden that was pressing down on my shoulders.'

They walked towards the door.

'Call if you're feeling lonely. I'll come over even if it's at night,' Said Rahmah.

'Won't Joe be angry?'

'Oh, he's changed now. He's afraid of me!' Rahmah said smiling.

'Thank God! I'm sure he's not afraid of anything else

other than losing your love!' said Sofia.

'Like losing his second wife?' asked Rahmah.

'No, he now understands what true love means. That love is only for you, not for other women,' said Sofia.

'But don't forget, I had to suffer before Joe discovered the love you mentioned,' said Rahmah going to her car.

Sofia watched the car driving out of the gates. She'd never realised that Rahmah's life had been filled with such suffering.

Sofia felt that there was still some hope for her, some chance to defend the happiness of her marriage. She felt braver. Come what may, Sofia now did not want to give up. She must do something and she must not admit defeat and allow her husband to bring another woman into her house.

Rahim was making a drink in the kitchen. Ah! He forgot to make ice last night. Fresh lemonade was not as delicious without ice. Rahim washed his hands. He could hear someone calling softly. The voice was getting nearer.

'Rahim! You're in the kitchen!'

Rahim opened the kitchen door. He found himself facing Khatijah, his sister.

'Why didn't you come in through the front door?' asked Rahim.

'I called out your name! You didn't hear me, I came to the kitchen. Are you cooking, Rahim?'

'No, kak! Come in! You shouldn't come in through the kitchen, it's quite dirty.'

'Oh it's alright,' said Khatijah.

'How did you come?'

'By taxi. I went to the clinic; I've got toothache.' Khatijah touched her cheeks. 'The doctor gave me pills.'

'Hmm, looks like it's going to have to be extracted!'

'That's for sure!'

Khatijah studied the kitchen. To see Rahim there made her sad. As the youngest child and the only boy in the family, he'd never had to work in the kitchen growing up.

'Would you like something to drink? There's no ice, I forgot to make some yesterday.'

'Ah, no need to make anything, Rahim. I'm here only to see you. I wasn't sure you'd be home.'

'If you had come earlier, I wouldn't have been. I just got back from playing football.'

'The People's Representative plays football too?' questioned Khatijah as she sat down on a stool.

'We have a game with the government office. We must practise or we'll lose. That'd be embarrassing!'

Rahim prepared black coffee for his sister. He knew that his sister liked black coffee. He took out the savoury shrimp dumplings from beneath the food cover.

'Let's go, why must we sit here?' Rahim beckoned his sister as he took the tray of food outside.

'Why trouble yourself over me!' said Khatijah. She tried to take the tray from Rahim but was prevented.

'You used to care of me,' Rahim headed toward the table. He placed the tray on the table.

'When did you make the shrimp dumplings?' She was also joking.

'When you arrived, wasn't I grilling them?' He also laughed.

The Wife

'Hmm ... still hot,' said Khatijah.

'That's right ... you never believe me!' said Rahim as he drank his lemonade.

Khatijah tasted the shrimp dumpings.

'Doesn't it hurt your tooth eating glutinous rice?' asked Rahim.

'But these dumpings are my favourite. And besides, right now I don't feel anything because I took pain killers earlier.'

'Sit down. I'll switch on the TV. I'm just going upstairs to change. I'm all sweaty after that football game. Do you know, I hadn't played for so long that it felt quite strange.'

Khatijah laughed. Rahim got up to switch on the TV, then went upstairs.

Khatijah looked round the living room. Poor thing, dust everywhere. I asked him to hire a maid, but he didn't want one. It is not that he's too lazy to clean the house but when does he have the time for that? He has to go to the office, go on visits, be busy with dinners that never stop?

If he lived near me, I could come once a week to help clean the house. But his house is too far away.

Rahim came downstairs to the living room. He saw that the television set was on but Khatijah was not watching it. She was busy washing up in the kitchen. Rahim switched off the television. He headed to the kitchen.

'Hey, why are you doing the dishes? I'll do them later!' said Rahim.

'I'm sorry to see you like this Rahim. You have to go to work, you have to come back and do housework, your food is not cooked! You know, if mother was still alive, she'd surely come and stay with you. I can't help you Rahim. I have kids and a husband; it's difficult!' Khatijah frowned and wiped her hands with a towel.

They left the kitchen.

'Please don't trouble yourself over me. I'm an adult with a family.'

'With a family, but where is your son? Where is your wife? It's no use having a family that's not living together. Do you know the difference between a child of your own and a child you care for? Do you remember Yam? She loved us more than she did her own siblings. Mother had cared for her since she was quite small. She didn't love her own mother at all, I think.'

'Yes, I know, but Hisham has to stay in the residential school.'

'Rahim, education is the same everywhere. The only thing is that you feel it's difficult to have him around because both of your work, that's all.'

'Yes, what can I do? It's not easy to find a maid these days.'

'That's why I said if mother was alive, she would be here taking care of her grandson. It makes me sad, Rahim. You used to be poor and mother took care of you. Now you have money but you have to do everything yourself.'

'Don't worry. Everything can be sorted out.'

They were quiet for a while.

'Well, what's the time now? I must go back! I wonder what's happening to my husband?' said Khatijah.

'Can't you even leave him for just a short while?'

'If I don't put food in front of him, he wouldn't eat. He'd rather go to the coffee shop. I don't really like him going there. It's usually hours before I see him again.'

'I thought of taking you to have fried noodles at the Rest House.'

'Ah, no need.'

'If so, I'm ready. Let me drive you home.'

'Just drive me to the taxi stand!' said Khatijah.

'Please! I'll see you home. No more arguments,' said Rahim firmly.

'Alright.' Khatijah knew that if Rahim had made up his mind, there was no point in protesting.

12

'**HEY** aren't you going to work today?' asked Asmah, seeing Nora lying face down on the bed.

'What about you, not going to work either?' asked Nora.

'Oh, I'm off today. I was on the late shift last night,' said Asmah. 'Why are you still curled up in a ball? You're not going to work?'

'I want to take leave, Asmah. Please help me get a medical note from Dr. Khalid. He'd surely give it to you since you're his nurse.'

'You're not ill,' said Asmah, somewhat tired with Nora's antics.

'Oh ... I don't feel like work today. I think I'll just quit my job. I'm tired of the new place.' Nora stretched out and looked at Asmah, who was facing the mirror.

'You can't take hardship. That's why you keep saying you'll quit. I'm poor, my mother had to sell dumplings to educate me after my father went away with another woman. I know the necessity of money. You can get money easily so you can show off. That's why you can quit your job,' said Asmah as she brushed her hair.

Nora was silent, not knowing what to say.

'What happened to that lover of yours?' Asmah asked as she turned to Nora.

'Him? The same!' said Nora.

'Hmm ... what is 'the same'? I heard once that you intended to marry him. How long do you plan on waiting for?' She turned round. 'He doesn't want to marry you and that's the truth. He's just fooling around. Taking you around everywhere, for what?'

'If there's no patience, there's no success.'

'Do you really think he'll marry you? Why would he want to marry you if he can already be with you like husband and wife as you're now?'

'Please watch your words.' Nora was beginning to get angry. She rose and sat at the edge of the bed hugging a pillow.

'I'm not afraid of reality. Why won't you face it? You're wasting your life. Men, what do they care? What's have they to lose? If the women are giving them everything for free, they'd be stupid if they didn't take the opportunity.'

'Please enough, enough. I don't want to hear anymore,' Nora shouted as loud as she could.

'Nora, please don't get upset with me. I'm only saying this for your own good. I know your parents are no longer alive and your relatives are far away. I'm also alone here. Who else will look out for us?'

'Why should I care? You yourself don't want to marry, why are you worried about other people who want to? You choose not to find a husband. That's your business, don't push your choices on me. I ... it's up to me what I want to do. You can also do what you like ... am I bothered?' Nora said getting up and placing her hands on her hips angrily.

'Alright then, don't you come crying and bitter to me later on,' said Asmah turning back to the glass. Now she was looking at Nora's reflection in the mirror in front of her.

'Me cry? Hah! Ha! Ha!' Nora laughed loudly. 'Halim is mine, why would I be crying? Ha! Ha! Ha!'

Halim walked toward the rented flat located near his office. As he was approaching the stairs, he saw Wati outside the next door bookstore. Wati also saw him.

'Halim!' Wati called out, walking toward Halim with a magazine in her hand.

Halim was surprised. He hadn't expected to see Wati in the neighbourhood.

'Where are you going?' asked Wati, pretending not to know Halim's secret.

'If I start talking, we'd be here forever. If you want to know, follow me, if you dare!' said Halim, as though challenging her. Wati took the challenge easily because she indeed wanted to see Halim's flat.

'You think you can scare me so easily? What should I be afraid of? Surely not you? You make me laugh!'

'What did you buy there?' asked Halim.

'I was looking for an article in the bookstore.'

'O.K., I'm moving along now!' said Halim, beginning to walk away.

'Ha! You're afraid!' Wati dared him.

'Come on! If you want to follow me, come on! But don't regret this, I've warned you,' said Halim, going up the stairs.

Wati knew Halim was going to his flat and she wanted to see it for herself. Wati followed Halim from behind.

'You're not afraid?' asked Halim climbing the stairs.

The Wife

'Afraid of what?'

'If it was night, at least no one might see!'

'Eh, what are you talking about?'

'This is the middle of the day!' said Halim. 'If you're following a man up to a room like this, and people see, isn't it dangerous?'

'I'm not doing anything!'

'Hmm, that's what you say, but what will others think?' asked Halim, as he turned smiling mischievously.

'I know what you're thinking; nonsense.'

They arrived upstairs and Halim put his hand in his pocket and took out a key. Wati waited. This was the flat Ahmad had described to her earlier.

Halim opened the door. 'Enter!' He touched Wati's hip and directed her through the opened door.

Wati stepped in slowly and tentatively. Her heart was pounding but she was feeling more curious than anxious.

The room was tastefully decorated with plenty of green plants everywhere. The terrazzo floor was covered with thick plush carpets. In the corner she noticed a huge basket filled with magazines and newspapers. Nearby there was a small console. A refrigerator stood in another corner.

'Whose place is this?' asked Wati, stunned.

'If it belonged to another person, would I dare to come in like this? Of course this is my place. I come to rest here whenever I feel tired,' said Halim.

'You rent this place?'

'Yes, is that wrong?'

'No.' Wati was silent for a moment. She studied a big painting with the lines that matched the colours of the cushions and plush carpet.

'The flat is nice, but why are there no chairs? No beds?' asked Wati watching Halim as he opened a window that looked out to the street.

'Don't ask too many dangerous questions! What would I want with a bed? If I lie on a bed, I would directly go to sleep until the next day. Ha! Then I would miss meetings and everything else.'

'I thought that if you needed to rest, you'd want a bed,' said Wati looking around, not knowing where to sit.

'When I'm here I take a bath. That freshens me up. After that, I read the newspaper for a while. Lately there's no time to read the newspaper. Work is piling up. If I'm hungry I ask Ahmad to bring food here.'

'Ahmad always comes here?'

'Yes, Ahmad comes here often, bringing whatever I want. There's also a telephone. Sometimes, I just call him.'

Wati headed for the cushions on the thick carpet.

'You'll find magazines there, you can read them. Drinks are in the refrigerator and maybe cookies too,' said Halim.

Wati reached for a magazine in the basket.

'Excuse me,' said Halim taking off his tie. He unbuttoned his shirt. He took it off. Wati appeared worried. 'I warned you earlier, and you said you weren't afraid,' said Halim with a mischievous smile.

Wati took a deep breath when Halim took a towel that was hanging near the sink and went to the bathroom. She was slightly apprehensive but she couldn't blame Halim entirely because she'd wanted to accompany him here. That was her best chance to see for herself the mysterioss flat described by Ahmad, and Wati had not wanted to miss the chance.

So, this is where Halim comes to calm his tired and restless soul. As she looked through the magazine, Wati's thought began to wander. Ahmad said Nora often came here. Perhaps not just Nora alone. Anyone could have come here: Aminah, Rogayah, Ahmad! Anyone. Others who I don't know perhaps, thought Wati.

Her thoughts was interrupted by the sound of footsteps from the cement stairs. The sound kept getting nearer. Halim's flat was on the top floor so the person must be intending to visit.

Perhaps, Ahmad is here, thought Wati. Ah it's alright, he'd probably think that I'm doing some work with Halim. Wati reached for the file on the table beside the basket and pretended to write.

The footsteps stopped at the door. Wati pretended to study the folder in her hand. She could hear someone trying to open the door but it was locked. Then she heard someone using a key. The knob turned. Wati looked around anxiously, heart pounding and filled with questions. She felt cold and frightened but she did not want to say anything. She only kept quiet and watched.

Nora was shocked to see Wati in Halim's flat. Wati pretended to be unruffled, but she was also just as startled. She'd never expected them to meet like this. Nora eyed Wati with growing anger. She did not care if the latter was a company executive or not. Wati tried to suppress her thumping heart, but it only beat faster.

'Nora! Come in.' Wati tried to break the silence, not knowing what else to say.

'Oh! Madam Fatimawati, you're here? I didn't expect to see a high person like you in a cheap place like this. I thought your taste, Madam Fatimawati, would be more for big hotels in Paris or Honolulu. If Halim brought me to Tokyo, he would surely bring Madam Fatimawati to more exotic places,' said Nora. She threw down her handbag on a table and it knocked over and broke a bowl. Nora was satisfied that she had broken something. Let other people know how crushed her heart was.

'Nora!' That was all that came out from Wati's mouth. She was shaken into silence. Her heart was beating faster. Her anger was beginning to rise.

'Madam Fatimawati, why are you surprised to see me? I also have a key to this place.' Nora dangled they key in front of Wati who was still sitting on the cushion.

'I never thought you and Halim....' Wati tried to respond, pretending not to know about their relationship.

'You didn't expect Halim and I to be lovers? You didn't know we were in Tokyo honeymooning with his wife? Hah! If he cared about his wife, would he have brought me along? And you, you're already the wife of a dignitary, and you're still having a fling with someone else?'

Wati felt there was no need to face such a foul mouthed and insolent woman. She reached for her handbag and headed for the door.

'Huh! You're afraid! Why are afraid to face me? Are you also afraid to face Sofia?'

Wati held the door knob but then stopped a moment and turned to Nora. She was trying to think of something to say until she heard the bathroom door open and Halim's voice calling her name. After that, she did not wait even a second longer before storming off. Her heart was raging.

Halim turned to Nora who stood fixed to the spot near the broken pot.

The Wife

'What happened?' asked Halim, as he walked out of the bathroom. 'Where's Wati gone?'

'How should I know!' Nora glanced at him sharply.

'What was the noise about?'

Nora ignored Halim's question. She had one of her own. What was Wati doing here?'

'Why do you need to know?'

'Oh, now I no longer need to know? You're a womanizer! How many women do you want? Your wife wasn't enough for you, and obviously I wasn't enough for you, so now you have that bitch!'

'Shut up! I refuse to listen to your slander. I don't want to be controlled or questioned. My own wife does not question me, so why should I listen to you? If you don't respect me as a human being, I don't need to respect you either. Men who're not respected are useless. Why should I entertain someone like you who doesn't know how to appreciate something?' Halim was furious. He put on his neck tie.

'Halim, I never thought you'd behave like this,' said Nora remorsefully.

'Huh! It's just too late. I'm sorry! You better go!' Halim looked at his wristwatch. 'I must too, I'm already late. And Nora, don't disturb me again. You've humiliated me enough. No more. Don't you think I know the truth? When we were in Tokyo, you called Sofia asking her to come down to the dance hall. You wanted to humiliate Sofia in front of everyone. I have been patient enough with you! I don't want to ever see your face again! Remember that!'

Halim turned and left. The door of the flat was slammed shut as hard as he could. His fury knew no bounds. Halim no longer cared what happened. If Nora decided to spread news of their affair to the whole world, let her. Let her!

Aminah and Rogayah looked at each other as they saw Wati coming into the office red faced. Wati did not look at them. She went straight into her room.

'Why didn't you tell her that the Honourable Mr Rahim has been waiting for her for such a long time?' Rogayah asked Aminah.

'I don't know! I was about to open my mouth but then she was gone. I didn't have time!'

'Poor Mr Rahim. If I had a husband like him I wouldn't let him wait that long.'

'Whenever he calls, Madam Wati is never in. I'm puzzled – do they live together like husband and wife?' said Aminah.

'I'm not surprised, if men can have two women, women can have the same thing too, can't they?'

'Eh, you're talking nonsense! Your husband has two wives, so what's your quarrel about?'

'My husband may well, but that's another story,' said Rogayah. 'His first wife is staying in the village, she didn't want to follow him to the city. He stays here four to five days and then goes back. I don't disturb his wife. I've got my own income, I work. Even if I wasn't working, it would be alright. But what would I do at home? It's better that I work; at least I can talk and laugh with you and Ahmad.'

'Yes, you're absolutely right,' said Aminah. 'No one who saw you would know you're married!'

'Where's the need to tell? As long as I'm not pregnant,

then it will stay a secret.'

'You seem happy with this secret life.'

Wati was seen leaving the office hastily. She was already late for a meeting. Mr Rahim did not come out.

'Rogayah, can you take a cup of coffee to Mr Rahim, I have to hurry. Thank you!' She left with a folder under her arm.

Aminah looked at Rogayah. Rogayah got up from her chair as she shrugged her shoulders. She pitied Mr Rahim, who had been there waiting for his wife.

'Aminah, I remember, he has not had his lunch yet.'

'He wanted to have lunch with his wife ... I think.'

'Poor thing!' Rogayah went into Wati's office.

'Mr Rahim, here's some coffee, Madam Wati asked me to bring it for you. Would you like to have anything to eat, Mr Rahim?' Rogayah looked at Mr Rahim who was holding the newspaper.

'Oh, sorry ... what's your name, miss?' asked Rahim, turning toward Rogayah.

'Rogayah!'

'Oh yes ... sometimes you answer the phone, right?'

'Yes, if Aminah's out. Err, what would you like to eat, sir?'

'It's alright. Don't trouble yourself.'

'It's nothing. The restaurant's just across the road. Ahmad, the office boy always goes there.'

'Oh, in that case, can you buy me some fried noodles?' asked Rahim.

Rogayah nodded and instructed Ahmad to go to the restaurant to get the food.

Nora regretted her actions. She'd never expected Halim to break off their relationship so easily. She had cried a lot. She had thought a lot. She realised that she was at fault. She realised that she'd been too jealous of Wati. She knew that Wati was someone's wife but the feelings of jealousy overcame everything else. Because of that jealousy she had now lost Halim.

Was that why Halim loved Sofia? Could it be that Sofia was not the jealous type? Sofia was patient with Halim's infidelity. Nora tried to be calm. She tried to overcome her sorrow. Now, Halim was gone from her life. Now, Nora was alone. Now, she realized how true Sofia's words were. Yes, Halim had found a new person, one who was not that young but was more elegant, and still attractive.

Nora remembered all of Asmah's advice, which at one time she had dismissed easily. She really hadn't expected Halim to easily break off their relationship. All her dreams were crushed.

Halim no longer wants to see me. Halim does not want me to contact Wati. Regardless of how much I'm suffering, I won't lower myself to beg Halim for his love.

I am ashamed, ashamed of myself. I am ashamed because I believed that Halim truly loved me, but now I'm discarded like an old rag. He used me to fulfill his wild desires and now he has left me with nothing. I have lost everything. Dignity. Self worth. Oh Sofia! She warned me. If I'd followed her advice, I wouldn't be suffering as I am now.

No matter, I won't return to Halim. I don't want a body

without a heart, I don't want love without sincerity. Sofia once told me that, even though she is Halim's wife. She advised me once.

Nora reached for the telephone. She dialed nine numbers. The telephone rang and then she heard a voice at the end other end. 'Hello!'

'Hello! This is Nora.'

'Yes?'

'I need to speak to you, Sofia...,'

'Why?' asked Sofia.

'Sofia....' Nora stopped as she realised she did not know what to say. Her mind was really entangled. She wanted to pour out her feelings to someone. She did not want to telephone Asmah. She knew Asmah would scold her.

'Nora ... what has happened?' asked Sofia.

'Sofia, Halim has left me, he does not want to have anything to do with me anymore.'

'Oh ... so? Why are you calling me then?' asked Sofia.

'I just want to let you know ... that what you told me was right. Halim cannot just look at an attractive woman. You yourself said so and warned me, but I didn't believe you. I never expected Halim to do this....'

'Oh, now he has found someone else?' asked Sofia. Her heart was pounding and she felt choked at the same time.

'I don't want to spread gossip. You'll find out for yourself, but I wanted to talk to you. I feel really disappointed,' said Nora, sadly.

'Nora, get a grip. Calm yourself. Try to look ahead, don't look back.'

'Sofia, I can imagine what you must have felt before. I really loved Halim. I couldn't think of anyone else then, but now, when I'm left with nothing, I can feel for you then. I'd like to ask for your forgiveness, Sofia.'

'Nora, I never really blamed you. It's just my luck that I married someone like Halim; what can I say? Remember, you're more fortunate than me. You found out Halim's character before you became his wife. You can forget him and erase him from your life. But I'm trapped because I'm already his wife. I can't get out of this golden cage.'

'Once you tried to advise me. Now it's my turn to tell you that Halim has another woman!' said Nora.

Sofia's heart was beating even faster. She tried to stop her head from spinning. She knew that Nora would not provide her with a name.

'Nora, you save yourself. You're still young, your future is still bright. Submit yourself to God. For me, life no longer has any meaning.'

'Forgive me, I've truly wronged you.'

'That's not your fault. You're still young, you don't know anything,' said Sofia.

'Thank you!' Nora put down the telephone.

She felt better after talking to Sofia. Something that had been constricting her chest had been released. Only Sofia truely understood her pain.

Ah! Halim! He's so conceited! He thinks that he's the only handsome and rich man in this world? He thinks that he has the right to conquer women; destroy their hopes? Huh! I don't want to destroy his future because that would lower me and mean victory for him. I don't want to see him win!

Yes, Sofia said I needed to look ahead. I'm luckier than Sofia because if Halim doesn't need me, I can find another to love. Not like Sofia who is trapped in the golden cage.

The Wife

Nora left Halim's flat with a calmer heart after talking to Sofia. She saw Ahmad crossing the road in front of her with a package in his hand.

'Ahmad!' Nora yelled.

Ahmad turned toward the voice that was calling him. He grinned, puzzled to see Nora. 'Hey, Nora! Don't you have any work; you're just going back and forth to Mr Halim's flat?'

'Ah, that's enough. That's an old story now,' said Nora. 'Where're you going with that package?'

'Well, the Honourable Mr Rahim is waiting to eat these fried noodles, I must hurry.' Ahmad began to move away from Nora but she followed him.

'Eh, you're following me, where're you going? You no longer work in our building.'

'Yes, I know...,' said Nora. 'I want to see Madam Wati.'

'For what?'

'To find another job. I'm tired of working over there!'

'All the men are bald!' said Ahmad, laughing.

'Yes, and you're not there!' Nora teased.

'Without you here we're rather lonely. Madam Wati isn't in, she's gone to a meeting. But if you want to find work, I think surely the Honourable Mr Rahim can help you,' said Ahmad.

'Ahmad, can you do something for me?'

'If you give me a treat!' said Ahmad grinning.

'Stewed noodles?'

'Watch a movie with me,' said Ahmad, smiling shyly.

'You're teasing me.' Nora pinched Ahmad's arm. They continued walking.

Even though I no longer want Halim, I should not lose this opportunity. If Wati can ruin mine and Halim's happiness, I can also expose her secret. This is my chance. Wati's husband is here now ... what am I waiting for?

Nora and Ahmad headed for the office. When they went in, Nora saw Aminah and Rogayah. She tried to smile. Ahmad went straight to Wati's office. Nora followed from behind.

'Eh, where does she think she's going?' Aminah whispered to Rogayah.

'I don't know Minah! Human behaviour is hard to predict, let alone understand.'

'Ehem....' Aminah smiled recalling Rogayah's secret earlier. Rogayah glanced sideways, also smiling.

Ahmad knocked on Wati's door.

'Come in.' A voice was heard from inside.

'Mr Rahim, this is Miss Nora, she wants to speak with you sir. This is the Honourable Mr Rahim Ahmad, husband of Madam Fatimawati,' said Ahmad.

Ahmad placed the package of fried noodles near a plate that was already there.

Nora held out her hand and Rahim got up to receive it. A Nora bad been pointed out to him once by Wati. But as he remembered, that Nora's hair was brown and curly.

'Nice to meet you,' said Nora.

'How are you?' asked Rahim sitting down again.

'I'm fine.'

'Please sit down,' said Rahim. Nora sat in a chair nearby. 'You wanted to see me miss? Is anything the matter?'

Nora looked at Rahim. The man was young and good-looking, not at all as she had expected.

'You're Madam Wati's husband!' The words blurted out from Nora's mouth.

'Why?' asked Rahim.

'I thought that if you're the Honourable ... you should be old and bald-headed.'

Rahim smiled.

'Not all the Honourables are bald,' said Rahim.

Nora smiled.

'Your Honourable is staying in Kampung Kaloi, is that right?' asked Nora.

'Yes, how do you know, Miss Nora?'

'Oh, I know Madam Wati; I know all her moves and steps.'

'What do you mean, Miss Nora?' asked Rahim, his heart beating fast. He was now sure that this was the Nora that Wati always mentioned.

There was a knock on the door. Rogayah came in with two cups of hot coffee. She placed them on the table. Nora tried to look the other way.

'Thank you, Miss Rogayah,' said Rahim.

Rogayah left.

'I'm trying to find work as a secretary,' said Nora, changing the subject.

'Work?'

'Yes, I cannot bear to stay here anymore. If possible, I'd like to go far, far away from here'

'You sound as though you're troubled!'

'Yes, since Madam Wati came here, I've been transferred to another building. Now, I'm really tired living in this city. If Your Honourable can help me.... I promise I'll help you.'

'Help me to do what?'

'If I can get another job!' Nora reminded him.

'Miss Nora ... about the job ... I'll try. About you helping me ... what help?'

'Madam Wati is an attractive person ... surely Your

Honourable doesn't want to lose her.'

'I don't understand you.'

'We have little time, I'm afraid Madam Wati might come back. This is her office, and you're her husband, sir.'

'It's better that you speak frankly,' said Rahim impatiently.

'Mr Rahim, you promise to find work for me ... wherever ... I don't want to stay here any longer. My heart is crushed.'

Nora tried to suppress her tears.

'Alright ... but explain to me what you have just said.'

'Yes, but promise?'

'I promise to find a job for you, Miss Nora ... wherever.' Rahim brought a business card. 'This is my card. One week from now, call me. *In-sha-Allah* I'll fulfil my promise.'

'Thank you.' Nora took the card and opened her bag. She placed the key on the table. She wrote on a piece of paper which she took from Wati's desk. She gave the paper to Rahim.

'This is the address. And this is the key. If you want to know, you can find out for yourself. I don't want to get involved any further. I have to go now, I don't want to run into Madam Wati.' Nora got up, her hand held out toward Rahim. Rahim shook it.

'Thank you. I'll call you in a week,' said Nora.

'Yes, this key and address?' Rahim turned but Nora was gone.

Rahim looked at the address on the piece of paper and the key on the table. He took them and studied the address. It was somewhere nearby.

Rahim was curious but didn't reallly suspect anything. Rahim knew that Wati was attractive. If Rahim was easily jealous, it would be difficult to live like this. Wife in the city, husband in the village. Rahim looked again at the address in his hand.

He had to leave for a meeting. He did not know how many hours he had been there in the room. His hungry stomach suddenly felt full. He looked at the unopened pack of fried noodles aand the two cups of Nescafe which had not been drunk.

Rahim did not have an appetite now. He looked at his wristwatch and then rose from his seat and left his wife's office.'

13

'**WHERE'RE** you going tomorrow?' asked Halim.

'I don't know yet. What're you doing?' Wati took a sip of her hot coffee and studied the dance floor.

'Well our work's finished now. If you want to look around, we could do that tomorrow. We've got a tourist guide.'

'If Datuk Kassim had come, he'd be spending the last day shopping for his wife.'

'And I would suffer, having to take him everywhere, choosing batik materials,' said Halim.

'That's why I said I didn't want to come. Sending a woman like me to Jakarta, it's a mistake!'

'If you hadn't come then who'd accompany me to play golf in the afternoon? Who'd dance with me in the evening?'

'When people come here, they don't play golf or go dancing!'

'And then, what do people do?' asked Halim smiling.

'Eh, women, what do I know!' said Wati.

The dance floor was lively and the music fast.

'Halim, how's Sofia?' asked Wati.

'Ah ... Sofia wants to live in her own world. I've tried to coax her several times, but she refused. What else can I do?'

The fast song was replaced with a slow number. Halim looked at Wati in her short, transluscent kebaya. He got up. 'Let's dance!'

Wati took his hand.

The Wife

'Wati...,' whispered Halim as he held her waist tightly. He was afraid that Wati could hear his heartbeat.

'Hmm?' Wati looked up; her cheek was close to Halim's.

'Why were you so wild back then at university?' asked Halim holding her closer.

'You were also wild!' said Wati, laughing.

'If I had tamed you then ... you wouldn't have become another man's wife.'

'You're such a womaniser ... I was frightened!'

'Are you afraid now?' asked Halim further, looking into Wati's eyes.

'No!'

'Why not?'

'You and I belong to other people.... So you can't do anything.'

'Do you think that's impossible?' asked Halim.

'Yes ... I think so, because your hands and mine are tied ... we cannot do anything!'

'But we're embracing now, aren't we?'.

'Yes ... we're embracing. But you see other people are also embracing,' said Wati, looking around.

'But, my heart is beating fast, Wati.' Halim whispered into Wati's ear. 'And I think I can hear that yours is too....'

Wati closed her eyes and tried to stop her heart from pounding. For a moment, she forgot everything. Oh Rahim, where are you? Why am I suddenly so frightened?

'You're trembling, Wati. Is something wrong?' asked Halim.

Wati stared at Halim. Impossible. Oh this was impossible. Wati tried to stop her mind from thinking further, but failed. She tried to stop her feelings, and that also failed. She stopped dancing.

'Halim, forgive me!' said Wati.

'What's wrong?'

'You know what,' said Wati. She realised she was still holding Halim's hand tightly.

They moved to the table.

'Would you like to leave?' asked Halim.

Wati nodded.

Halim still did not let go of Wati's hand. They walked to the swimming pool which was illuminated by the light of the crescent moon. Two or three lights shone at the corners of the pool.

They stopped walking. Halim's hand now rested on Wati's waist.

'We're too anxious. Maybe we should take a dip to cool down!' Halim whispered.

'Is that allowed?' Wati allowed Halim's hand to rest on her waist. She was aware that this was strange but for some reason she didn't want to object.

Halim pointed to a corner of the hotel.

'That's your room and that's my room. Do you want to change into swimming gear?' asked Halim.

Wati liked swimming but not in the middle of the night like this. Before she could decide Halim had left. She hesitated a moment and then went to her room to change.

When she came back, Halim was already in the pool. Wati joined him, swimming up and down in the moonlight. Suddenly she felt someone grab her leg and she twisted round to see Halim.

'Aren't you afraid?' asked Halim.

'Afraid? Afraid of you?'

Halim laughed.

'Is your heart still nervous?' he asked. 'Feel my chest.' He reached for Wati's hand and placed it on his chest. 'What do you feel? Still beating fast?'

'I can feel a heartbeat so at least we know that you're not dead, ' said Wati lightly.

Halim threw his head back and laughed.

Nora picked up the telephone. 'Hello! This is Nora! Can I speak to the Honourable Mr Rahim Ahmad?'

'Oh, Miss Nora. This is Rahim!'

'Good morning. I called yesterday, but couldn't get through.'

'How're you?' said Rahim.

'I'm well! How about you, Mr Rahim?'

'Good too. About the job that you requested, there's one, but....'

'But what? Mr Rahim, you promised ... promises must be kept,' said Nora.

'Patience Nora, I do remember my promise. There's someone looking for a secretary but you must work in France...'

Nora screamed. 'France!'

'How's that? Agreed?'

'Really? France? Yes, I agree!'

'If so, call this number, 767074 and ask for Puan Sri Salmah.'

'Alright ... thank you!' said Nora.

'Tell Puan Sri Salmah that I asked you to call.'

'O.K. Thank you, Mr Rahim. Thank you so much. When I'm in France I'll send you a postcard, sir.'

Nora put down the telephone. France! She smiled to herself.

She hadn't mentioned the key. She'd been tempted to ask but had made a promise to herself: there was to be no more looking back.

There was a car honking outside the house. Sofia hurriedly headed towards the gates and opened them. A white car was stopped there. The left door opened; Rahmah stepped out. The car engine was still on.

'Oh Rahmah. Wow! Come in,' said Sofia approaching the white car.

'Sofia, you know Dr. Subardi, don't you?' asked Rahmah turning to look at the driver of the car.

'Oh, Dr. Subardi! I didn't see you just now. Come in!'

'I've some work. My house is not tidy and Joe will be arriving. If you don't mind, bring Rahmah along later.'

'Are there any kuih?' asked Rahmah.

'We'll just buy some!' said Dr. Subardi.

Rahmah closed the door. Dr. Subardi continued on toward his house.

Sofia and Rahmah headed for the chairs near the fountain under the trees.

'Where were you?' asked Sofia.

'At home. Subardi dropped by earlier. Joe said he wanted to

go over to Subardi's house, something he wants to see there ... I don't know. So, I thought I'd take the opportunity to come and see you. If I came with Joe, you know, everything must be so quick. This way we can have a proper chat.'

'Let's go in. We'll have something to drink.'

'No need. I want to slim down a bit. Well, this body, I've tried everything. Nothing works,' said Rahmah holding her hips.

'How's Datin Zaharah?' asked Sofia.

'She went to London recently with her husband. Well, they're wealthy, so she can go with him everywhere. Someone like me can only afford to go to Subardi's house!' Rahmah laughed wholeheartedly.

'That's why you're not thin. You're always happy.'

'I hear your husband Halim is in Jakarta. Why didn't you go along?'

'I can't be bothered. I don't want a repeat performance.'

'What happened with that woman?'

'Oh yes! Do you know? She telephoned me recently! She said Halim has left her. But she also said...' Sofia stopped and looked away.

'What is it? What did she say now?'

'She said Halim has another woman.'

'If that's so, don't worry. Men only want to fool around. Look at her, she was ditched. Ah ... let it be, this one will also be ditched soon. Trust me.' Rahmah slapped Sofia's thigh.

'How was the last meeting?' asked Sofia.

'Sofia, since I heard them gossiping about you, I can't be bothered to go there. It's better that I go to the mosque to hear a talk. There, it's always sniping. Did you go?'

'You know what, Rahmah? Last week, I braved myself to

go. Ha! I went! I wanted to see what they'd say! At first, I could see they'd expected me to show up all troubled and tearful. They do like to see people in trouble.'

'Ha and then, what happened?' Rahmah touched Sofia's thigh, barely able to hide her curiosity.

'I told them a pack of lies! I told them what I bought, what Halim bought for me and I also mentioned that woman's name Nora. I said we went everywhere shopping together!' said Sofia.

'Did they believe you?'

'I told them fantasies. These people all do that. If I admitted defeat, they'd only think I was stupid. Yes, I think I really fooled them. I said Halim was too busy to take me shopping so he brought his office colleague along to keep me company. When Halim was attending a meeting, we went here and there with all the other tourists!'

'Well, you are a one!' Rahmah laughed.

'And I didn't forget to tell them I came home first and Wati picked me up at the airport. I had to come back earlier because my grand aunt in the village had passed away!'

'That was why you were crying at the airport!' Rahmah laughed again. 'You're very good at lying. Your grand aunt is long gone!'

'Ah, now I'm getting good at telling lies! I've learned to lie. And with people like them, there cannot be sincerity. They use us. We must learn to be like them ... talk like them too.'

'Did they believe you?'

'What do I care if they believed me or not? After what they've told us, do you believe them?'

'I don't know ... I really don't know!' said Rahmah.

'I couldn't care less what they thought! I only wanted to

release my anger!'

'Do you want to be like them?'

'Rahmah ... should we bleat when we are in the sheep pen....'

'If it's a buffalo, you moo!' added Rahmah.

'Yes ... we need to continue living! Personally, I don't want to go there ever again. They've nothing better to do than talk about others!' Sofia paused for a moment and then changed the topic. 'By the way, where's Subardi's wife? I've never seen her.'

'I don't dare ask Subardi. People say that she left for her country. Other people said that she asked for a divorce ... if we ask other people, the story might be different.'

'I'm sorry to hear that!' said Sofia.'What about their children?'

'There's one living with Subardi's grandmother in Surabaya. Let's go to Subardi's house. You shouldn't be sitting here alone with your husband so far away. Come with me, it's alright.'

'Are you leaving now?'

'Yes.'

'You're changing your outfit?'

'Ha ... why not... if Joe is in the right mood, I can ask him to treat me to some satay at the lakeside stall there!'

'O.K. I'll change first. We can bring the roasted glutinous rice which I prepared earlier,' said Sofia, getting up.

'You prepared glutinous rice to eat all by yourself?'

'It's silly but I was thinking about my son and how much he loves to eat glutinous rice. Today his letter arrived you see. There's nothing much for me to do, so I made the glutinous rice. I gave a little to Datin Jamilah who lives over there.'

'Go and get ready ... I want to look at your orchids. I'll wait here.'

'Malisa, what's wrong with you; are you ill? You're always so quiet lately.' said Rokiah.

Malisa, who was sitting on the steps looking out at the road, shook her head. 'I'm fine, Rokiah.'

'When's Wati coming back? She's always abroad.'

'She's working, isn't she?'

'She must be buying a lot of batik. Did you order some?' asked Rokiah arranging the shoes that were out of place.

'No! You're all dressed up. Where're you going?'

'To a friend's place. Bye!'

Malisa nodded weakly and sat back to watch Rokiah walking out. She was feeling anxious. It had been a while since she'd been back to her hometown. Perhaps, that explained her anxiety. Rahim used to offer to drive her there but often Malisa couldn't go because she didn't have fixed a work schedule.

She thought of Rahim's handsome face with his hair falling halfway down his forehead. Then she tried not to think about the handsome face, but that was more difficult.

When they'd first met, Malisa had accepted Rahim as a casual acquaintance. He was, after all, a married man. But now, each time Rahim came and Wati could not be with him, Malisa was the one who prepared his food.

Initially, that was the only thing Malisa thought she could do but now after quite a while since the last time Rahim was

202

there, she felt a longing for him.

Malisa tried to suppress her feelings. She tried to remind herself that she was thinking of someone else's husband. Could this be what people call love? Malisa had never felt this way before. She was afraid. Why someone else's husband? Why must he be someone else's husband? She buried her face in her hands and sobbed.

She remembered when they had sat talking that night. She could still feel Rahim's embrace.

He thought I was his wife. But after he knew I was not Wati, he still did not release my hand, why? Ah, no it did not mean anything. Rahim was only feeling frightened at the time. He had a bad dream. He was holding my hand tightly only to calm himself down. It could be that I was disturbing him at a critical moment in the dream. Perhaps he was startled and that that was why he hugged me tightly and did not want to let go of my hand afterwards. Oh Rahim! What should I do now? Malisa did not realise that Rahim's Mercedes was driving in slowly into her house yard.

She heard the closing of the car door. Before she could get away, Rahim was approaching, calling to her. 'Malisa! Why are you crying?'

Malisa did not dare to look up because she did not want Rahim to see her tears. She hadn't expected Rahim that day. She remained sitting.

'Malisa!' She could hear Rahim's gentle voice and then she felt his hand touching her neck. She was afraid to face Rahim. She was afraid to look at his face. She was afraid Rahim could read the secret content of her heart.

Rahim sat down beside her. Now Malisa could feel Rahim's thigh touching hers. Malisa was afraid to move. She was afraid to take her hands off her face.

'Why are you crying, Malisa? There must be a reason. You had an argument with Rokiah, is that right?' Rahim tried to guess.

Malisa shook her head.

'I came to pick up something that I'd left behind. I know Wati isn't here, she called from Jakarta,' said Rahim.

'Oh!' said Malisa.

'I didn't come from Kaloi. I had a meeting in the city earlier. So ... after the meeting I came straight here.'

Malisa stood up and walked over to the tap. She pretended to wash her hands. She could feel Rahim coming nearer behind her. Malisa could feel Rahim taking a deep breath near her ear. Malisa remained fixed. Her heart raced again.

'Malisa....' Rahim touched Malisa's shoulder slowly.

Malisa froze. Not a word came out of her mouth.

'Malisa....' Rahim said again.

Malisa turned to Rahim. She had suppressed the longing for a long time and now Rahim was in front of her. She turned to look at Rahim and tried to stop her tears. She closed her eyes and the tears flowed down her soft cheeks.

She could feel Rahim's fingers brushing the tears away.

'There's something you refused to tell me ... something that's troubling your heart,' said Rahim.

Malisa held Rahim's fingers that were wiping her tears. She held them tightly ... then let them go slowly.

'I would like to help, Malisa...' said Rahim, as Malisa turned away and walked into the kitchen.

'Rahim, you cannot help me,' she said. 'Even I cannot help myself. That's what's making me sad.' She sat down on a stool near the table in the kitchen. She had a faraway look.

The Wife

Rahim went nearer to Malisa. He sat near the table, his thigh near Malisa's arm. Malisa looked up at him. 'Rahim you're the people's representative, a powerful man. You can help other people, but not me.'

'Do you have a broken heart, Malisa?' asked Rahim. His right hand touched Malisa's head.

'Yes, I'm heartbroken ... I've lost hope ... my future is completely void.'

'Who's that stupid ... one who doesn't know how to appreciate you ... who's that stupid human being?' asked Rahim.

Oh Rahim, you do not know how I am suffering thinking about you who belongs to someone else; you should not be here with me like this. You should not be comforting me like this. You belong to someone else. I have no right to feel so sad about my empty future, without you.

'I'm disappointed Rahim. Disappointed because I've chosen wrongly. I know he can never return my love, but ... but I still love him. That's my regret. I've fallen in love with someone who cannot respond to my love,' said Malisa. She felt strangely relieved to pour out her feelings and hardly realised that she had buried her face in Rahim's thigh at the table. She couldn't stop crying as Rahim caressed her hair.

'Malisa, you're such a special person ... I'll do anything. If possible, to help you ... but what can I do ... I don't know how to help you. I don't want you to be crushed. I don't want to see sweet Lisa with her dimples go through life with a broken heart! Malisa ... how can I help you?'

Malisa and Rahim did not realise Rokiah had quietly entered the house. Rokiah knew Rahim was there because she had seen the Mercedes parked outside. Rokiah went straight to the kitchen to get a drink and then she stopped. She saw Malisa crying in Rahim's lap. Rokiah no longer felt thirsty. Instead, she went to her room. She suddenly realised why Malisa had been so subdued.

Since that night Malisa had felt only anguish. She knew she was facing a dead end. She could not sleep at night. There was no solution to her problem. Malisa could no longer look at Rahim for hear her secret would be known. What should she do?

It was not possible for Rahim to love her because Rahim was already taken. Malisa didn't wish to destroy Rahim's marriage. She did not want to hurt anyone. Let her suffer alone. Let the wound cure by itself.

I should just let go. As long as I see Rahim's attractive smile, his jokes, his gaze, I'll suffer in my heart. I'll be buried in this suffering.

I should just go. Far away so that Rahim's face would not haunt me.

She heard Rokiah coming out of her room.

'I'm leaving now, Malisa!' Rokiah shouted, not realising that Malisa was already outside.

'Oh! You're packed! Where are you going with all these bags?' Rokiah looked at Malisa's luggage arranged beside the door.

'Rokiah, I have to leave!'

'Where're you going?'

'Forgive me, I can no longer stay with you and Wati.'

The Wife

Malisa looked like she had been crying.

'Malisa....' Rokiah went and sat in a chair beside her.

Malisa wiped her eyes.

'What's wrong, Malisa?'

'Nothing's wrong. I'm going to stay with my cousin in Meranti Road. Forgive me...' added Malisa.

'Are you upset with me?' asked Rokiah.

'No, I think it's better that I just leave. I feel guilty staying here.'

'Guilty in what way?'

'Ah, I'll tell you about it some other time. You're already late for work. This is my new address. I'll come back to get the rest of my stuff.'

Malisa held out a piece of paper to Rokiah, who took it. 'Forgive me, Rokiah. Thank you for everything. Do come and see me.'

'Malisa, I never thought you'd leave like this....' Now it was Rokiah's turn to cry. She hugged Malisa. 'If you go ... I will be lonely!'

'Don't worry, Rokiah. I'll not cut you off. We'll see each other often.'

'You don't want to talk about it with me?'

'Someday,' said Malisa. 'Goodbye, Rokiah.' Malisa rose. She heard a car honking outside.

'Your friend's here!' said Rokiah and got up.

They hugged each other again.

'Take care of yourself, Malisa...'

Rokiah helped Malisa to carry her bags to the waiting car. She looked at her friend through eyes full of tears.

14

THERE was a knock on the door.

'Come in,' said Rahim. He stopped writing. He had never before seen the office boy who was standing at the door.

'Come in...,' said Rahim again.

'The Honourable Mr Rahim?' The office boy asked. There was a large envelope in his hand.

'Yes!'

'I was instructed to deliver this to you, sir.' The office boy held out the large envelope to him. Rahim took it with both hands.

'Alright, thank you,' said Rahim, placing the envelope on the table.

The office boy nodded and left the room.

Rahim opened the large envelope, looked inside and couldn't believe what he saw. His heart was pounding. He was shocked beyond words. He felt sad and angry all at once. It was unexpected, unthinkable.

Impossible! Impossible! But isn't the evidence clear and decisive? Rahim still refused to believe it.

He buried his face in his hands. His heart was pounding. He felt the world had suddenly been drained of substance. He took a long deep breath but his chest still felt suffocated.

The telephone on the table rang. Rahim did not want to answer it, but it kept on ringing. He picked up the receiver.

'Hello!'

'Hello! Your Honourable!'

'Yes,'

'Have you received the envelope, sir?'

'Yes, I have ... alright, thank you. I'll call you later.' Rahim placed the telephone back on the receiver.

He called Fatimawati at her office but she was not in. Then he left a message with Rogayah that he was coming over. Fatimawati should wait for him at her office. After that, he instructed his secretary to cancel all his appointments for the rest of that day.

Rahim grabbed his car keys, picked up the envelope and headed for his Mercedes. Getting in, he slammed the car door as hard as he could. He started the engine and it roared roughly. Hastily he moved the car out of the garage, and he paid no attention when a loud bang suggested that he'd hit something.

Rahim accelerated towards the main road. No matter how fast he drove it could not eliminate the pain in his heart. He felt bitter to the bone. He pressed the accelerator again. The car sped along. He still hoped that speed could blast away all the feelings that were threatening to overwhelm him, but his thoughts were racing too. He couldn't get a hold on his feelings.

I need to see Wati, I need to clarify everything. Only Wati can give me an explanation. I do not care about what anyone else says, only Wati.

Wati! What if she is unable to explain? What if she can't say anything to calm my anxieties? I do not care about everything else. I only want her to answer my one question. Does she still love me? That is all I want to know. That is all! I know without her my life is empty. I know that whatever happens, I am still hers. I must hear it from her. I want the sincere and honest truth . I know she has never lied to me before. Never!

Rahim had never driven that fast. He drove without giving thought to what was in front of him. Still he felt the car was taking too long to get to the city.

After watering the orchids, Sofia went inside. She had not tidied her bedroom. She knew that if she didn't make her bed that day, next day it would be worse. She recalled that Halim had played golf the previous afternoon and that his clothes were still in the golf bag.

Sofia wiped her hand with the towel near the sink. She headed toward Halim's golf clubs. Usually the golf bag was placed together with the golf clubs beside the stairs.

Sofia unzipped the bag and took out everything from it. There were drawer keys, socks, golf balls, a bottle of cream and a lipstick. She studied the last two items. She had never seen Halim using these things! But, Sofia knew that she had seen the bottle before. Yes, she herself had bought in Tokyo, Wati's face cream. What was Wati's face cream and lipstick doing in Halim's golf bag?

Sofia was aware that sometimes Wati came by to fetch Halim. Supposedly they were going to the same meeting, but after that, what? Ah! Sofia did not want to know more about it. She had once promised that she would not heed Halim anymore. Sofia studied the bottle of cream again. This was certainly Wati's cream. How had the bottle of cream got in

Halim's golf bag? Nora had told her that Halim had a new woman! Sofia never suspected then that the woman might be her friend, someone who had once shared the same pillow and bed with her.

Wati! Wati who had gone to great lengths to help Sofia so that Halim would not be attracted to other women. Wati who sympathised with Sofia when she found out that Halim was still cheating on her! Wati the best friend who had seemed ready to do anything to help save Sofia's and Halim's marriage. Ah, Wati!

Sofia breathed deeply and picked up the phone.

'Madam Fatimawati? This is Madam Sofia, Mr Halim's legal wife,' said Sofia.

'Eh, Sofia ... I didn't know it was you ... how're you?' said Wati.

'Did you want to try and fool me all along?'

'Why am I hearing an angry tone? Is there anything wrong?'

'... Don't pretend with me. I know now that you're the enemy from within ... you're the wolf in sheep's clothing!'

'What are you talking about, Sofia?'

'That's enough ... don't pretend. You think I'm not aware that you're cheating with my husband?'

'Sofia!' Wati tried to protest.

'Wati ... don't try to hide. What did you advise me once? Don't give a chance to those cheap women. Yes, I'm following your advice now. Do you think I will give you a chance? If I were you, Wati, I'd be thankful to have a husband like Rahim who's patient and sincere, but you took advantage of his honesty. You're not faithful to him either!' Sofia could no longer contain all her feelings. It was the time and place for her to pour out everything that she needed to.

'Sofia ... perhaps you've misunderstood! I never meant to take Halim away from you. Never.'

'Wati ... I don't care anymore. Whatever happened, happened. Anyway, my love for Halim is long dead and buried. But don't imagine I'll move out from this house of pain, even if it kills me. I'll not budge an inch. I'll not move out as long he does not divorce me,' said Sofia determinedly.

She put down the telephone and walked away. Wati however was still holding the telephone. She was still saying Sofia's name. Slowly, she placed the telephone down and closed her eyes. The pounding of her heart would not cease.

Sofia's bitter words rang in her ears. I never thought Sofia would turn on me. Oh Sofia! Why Sofia! Why? I really never had any intention to snatch her husband away. Not even once.

Wati already knew that Rahim was on his way to see her. But she must face Halim first. This matter could not be put off. Halim needed to know what his wife had said to her. Halim needed to face up to things.

Wati got up, took her her handbag and went out of her office, heading toward Halim's. She saw Ahmad leaving Halim's office with a file.

'Mr Halim just left, Madam Wati. He went to his flat. He asked me to bring this file over to him,' said Ahmad.

'Let me bring the file to him. This is urgent. I need to see him now, it can't be delayed' said Wati, seriously.

Ahmad handed the file to Wati.

Wati took the file and left the office. She must see Halim at once, if not she felt she would explode. Her anger was no longer within her control.

212

The Wife

How could Sofia say all those hurtful words? If I knew Sofia would behave so judgementally, I would not have bothered being her friend!

Now Nora is gone, disappeared without a trace. Halim is already tamed, no longer going out at night. What else does Sofia want? Halim was right; Sofia has changed. What do I get from watching over a womaniser like Halim? I followed him here and there ... afraid that he would hook up with other women. Did Sofia thank me? No, in fact I was accused of stealing her husband. Why would I want to steal her husband? I am already married!

Hastily, Wati climbed the stairs to Halim's flat. She knocked on the door a few times. Moments later she heard someone approaching the door and opening it;

'Hey, you're brave to open the door clad only in a towel.' said Wati.

'I thought it was Ahmad. I asked him to come earlier, to bring a file. At 2.30 I have a meeting in Putera Building. Come in.' Halim's body was still wet.

Wati locked the door. She went straight to the cushions and threw her keys on the carpet.

'What's wrong, Wati?'

'Halim ... Sofia called me. She was talking nonsense!' said Wati.

'What did she say?'

'She said I was trying to steal you away from her.'

'Ah Sofia! I don't know what to do with her.'

'What should I do?' asked Wati.

Halim looked at Wati. He was also lost for ideas. 'What did she say to you?'

'Well ... I'm not good at telling stories, but her words

hurt me,' said Wati.

For the first time, Halim realised that Wati crying. Wat who he had never seen succumb to tears, was sobbing. '] never thought Sofia would be that hard hearted ... I never expected her to behave that way...'

Halim went nearer to Wati. He stroked her shoulder, trying to console her. 'Be patient, Wati. Perhaps Sofia was jus venting. She has been patient long enough, she has suppressed her anger long enough...'

'But is this fair? She's angry with Nora but why does she turn on me? Sofia doesn't know how hard I've worked to bring you two closer again. Sofia doesn't know that I've sacrificed for her. She doesn't know!' said Wati, crying again

'Ah, why do you have to think of Sofia? She doesn't think of us anymore. She only thinks about herself. She's too stubborn. I've asked forgiveness from her but she remains aloof. How long am I expected to stay in the house feeling guilty all the time? '

'I never thought that all this while she doubted me!' said Wati regretfully.

'Wati, I'm sorry for Sofia's insolent behaviour. I'm the one who's wrong. Because of me, you're enemies with Sofia ... your own friend.'

'The one who's wrong is not you, Halim, but me ... thought I could solve your marital problems. I was mistaken but now there's no use regretting.'

'Wati, I've no regrets. I don't regret any of the time we spent together. I've been patient long enough with Sofia who's so stone-hearted. She has tortured me enough. Don't you realise that I feel happy with you beside me each moment When I go home, my life is empty: without words, withou laughter. I can no longer bear to live like this,' said Halim.

'But Halim, you know we were only together because of the situation.'

'Well I'm grateful for the situation because you bring joy to my life. You're the music in my empty life. If you were not married, I'd have pleaded with you, and kidnapped you,' said Halim.

Rogayah was ready to go out to lunch. Aminah was not at work. She had already been off sick for two days. Roagayah wondered why Madam Wati had left in such a hurry when she'd already been told that Mr Rahim was coming. Rogayah saw Ahmad passing by.

'Ahmad! Madam Wati, where was she going?'

'She ... a ... she ... a ... ah!' Ahmad tried to lie but was not good at it.

Rogayah's sight shifted elsewhere. The Honourable Mr Rahim had arrived. Ahmad quickly left. Rogayah had to think fast.

'Mr Rahim! You want to see Madam Wati, right?' Rogayah knew it was a silly question, but she could not think of anything else to say.

Rahim's face was the same as always but Rogayah sensed he was upset. He headed toward Wati's room without answering her. Rogayah hastily followed him from behind, trying to salvage the situation.

'Mr Rahim....' Rogayah went into Wati's room. Rahim was still standing frozen in front of Wati's desk. He looked anxious.

'Where's Madam Wati?' Rahim turned to look at Rogayah, seriously.

'I've already informed her that you wanted to see her. But I saw her leaving. She must have just popped out for a minute.'

'She knew that I wanted to see her? But she couldn't wait even for a short while!' said Rahim.

Rogayah was quiet. She had never seen Rahim this furious. Before Rahim could say anything, Rogayah left. She did not want to answer Rahim's questions anymore. Something terrible must have happened.

Rahim sat in the chair in front of the small table. He was silent, still. His heart was fuming: I have been patient long enough ... too long. Wati does not appreciate my trust and love. She does not take this marriage seriously.

He put the large envelope on the table.

Rogayah knocked on the door to bring in a glass of lemonade. Perhaps this would cool down Rahim a little. She placed the drink on the table and invited Rahim to have some. Rahim drank the lemonade and thanked her. Rogayah then left him there alone. Wati's door was not closed completely and Rahim could hear the conversation between Rogayah and Ahmad. He heard Ahmad mentioning Kerabu Road. He remembered the address Nora had given him and took out his wallet to find it. Yes, that was it! Kerabu Road. He got up quickly and left Wati's office without explaining to anyone. He was really furious.

Flat number 3125, Kerabu Road ... yes this was the address. And this was the key. Rahim climbed the stairs. Outside the flat he put his hand in his pocket. He was nervous but he steeled himself as he took out the key Nora had given him. Slowly, Rahim placed the key in the lock and turned the knob. Slowly he opened the door and looked inside.

Quickly he closed the door again. He did not want to see anymore. What he had seen and heard were enough. What more proof did he want? What other hurtful evidence? He ran down the stairs and headed toward his car.

He was angry beyond words ... it seemed that life was dark.

The Mercedes turned into Seroja Road. Suddenly he had a strong urge to show the pictures to Malisa and Rokiah ... The gates were open so he drove straight into the house yard.

'Rahim!' greeted Rokiah. 'Come in!'

'Where's Malisa?' Rahim asked, before even reaching the front door.

'Come in first...,' said Rokiah, looking dejected.

'Why are you crying Rokiah? I can see your eyes are swollen!' said Rahim, as he entered. He sat in a chair.

Rokiah also sat down facing Rahim.

'She's no longer living here.'

'Why not?' Rahim was startled.

'She didn't explain. She said she felt guilty staying here!'

Rahim was silent, he felt the emptiness of the house without Malisa's sweet voice greeting him.

'She is tortured, Rahim ... because the man she loves cannot reciprocate her love. Even though she has never told me who that person is, I know. That's why she doesn't want to stay here anymore. She's afraid to face him often ... she doesn't want her heart to be continuously crushed because her love is not returned.'

'Rokiah?'

Rokiah wiped the tears from her eyes.

'Could it be she's...?' Rahim asked.

Rokiah could read what was on Rahim's mind. She nodded.

'Rahim ... Malisa kept her love a secret because it's you; because you're a married man.'

'Rokiah!' Rahim looked squarely at Rokiah. 'I've also tried ... I've tried to forget her but it was in vain. I also wanted to keep my love a secret even to myself because I'm already married. But ... look at this.' Rahim gave the envelope to Rokiah.

Rokiah took the envelope. She was shocked to see Wati's pictures.

'Wati! Where did you get these?'

'My friend is a private investigator. He has contacts everywhere ... even in Jakarta. I have a certain dignity to maintain as a public person. These pictures could threaten my position. I'm afraid they could even be used to bring me down one day. Hmm, Rokiah ... where's Malisa? I need to see her.'

'When?'

'Right now. Can you take me...?'

'Yes, Rahim ... I can. I know where she lives.'

Malisa regretted falling in love with a married man but what could she do; it had happened. Perhaps she would meet another man ... perhaps one day she would marry ... but this would not wipe the sweet memories that had been planted in her heart.

She was sitting on the swing beneath a shady tree. She

couldn't stay in this place longterm because it was too far from where she worked. Her cousin was staying with her friends. Malisa felt sad. She closed her eyes. Her whole face was covered with her two hands. She could still see Rahim in the space between her eyes. She could still feel herself crying in Rahim's lap. As if her head was caressed slowly by Rahim. As if Rahim was uttering her name.

'Oh ... Rahim ... where are you?' The question was blurted without Malisa realising it.

'I'm here....' She heard Rahim's voice.

Could she be dreaming? Malisa opened her eyes. Dimly she could see a shape, as though Rahim was standing in front of her. Oh ... I must be dreaming, Malisa thought again.

'Malisa....' She heard her name again. She felt someone touching her hand. She closed and opened her eyes again. 'Is it you Rahim? Is it true, or am I dreaming?'

Rahim sat down beside her on the swing and clasped Malisa's hand.

'Look at me Malisa...,' said Rahim.

Malisa turned. It was true, she was beside Rahim. Her heart pounded hard. She could not believe it. She thought she was dreaming. But no, Rahim who she was missing so badly was truly beside her now.

'How did you find me?' asked Malisa, tightly gripping Rahim's hand.

'Even if you had ran to the edge of the land, I'd follow you,' said Rahim.

'Rokiah ... yes Rokiah!' Malisa recalled that she had left her address with Rokiah.

'She's waiting in the car at the end of the road there. She didn't want to come in.'

'Why did you come to find me Rahim? Even if you say you want to help me, there's no remedy for my illness.'

'Malisa...,' Rahim held Malisa's shoulder. 'Look at me.'

Malisa turned. Her chest felt very tight now. Rahim was looking into her eyes.

'What's wrong?' she asked.

'Could you love me?'.

'Why do you ask me this impossible question, Rahim?'

'Because I'm afraid of losing you. My life would be empty without you, Malisa. My life would be lonely.'

'But you're already married. She should fill all the emptiness in your life,' said Malisa, looking at the clouds that were parading by slowly.

'You yourself know that Wati doesn't have time for me in her life. Since I met you, my life has become meaningful'

Malisa began to cry. 'I never thought you could love me!'

'And I never imagined that you loved me!' said Rahim.

'Rahim, you shouldn't have come here. Actually we should just be saying goodbye now,' said Malisa, her tears flowing down again.

'Malisa ... I'd like you to tell me sincerely,' said Rahim. He held Malisa's hand tightly. 'Would you be able to forget me ten years from now?'

'Even if it was a thousand years, Rahim, I'll never forget you. My world is empty without you.'

'If so, come with me to Kaloi. Accept me as your husband. I promise that I'll make you happy. I'll not neglect you.'

Malisa's heart was in turbulence. She had never thought, never expected....

'But what about Wati? I don't want to destroy your bliss.'

'Why do you want to remind me of Wati?'

The Wife

'I'm afraid...' said Malisa.

'Malisa ... quit your work and come with me to Kaloi; stay with me. I need a wife like you, a wife who'd take care of my needs. I need you by my side, always.'

'What about Wati?' asked Malisa.

'I don't want to think about Wati now. What I know is that I don't want to lose you again.'

'Rahim ... I'm afraid!' said Malisa.

'What are you afraid of, my love? Say it ... are you afraid of me?' asked Rahim. 'I'm the one who's afraid ... I'm afraid that you will run away again.'

Malisa was silent.

'Malisa...' said Rahim again. He leaned forwards and whispered in her ear: 'We'll marry tonight!'

Malisa was even more shocked. 'Don't joke about marriage, Rahim.'

'No, Malisa. I'm not joking. Let's marry this very night. I don't want to be without you even for a second,' said Rahim.

'I need to think.'

'If you love me, you'll not think about it anymore. You know yourself that I want you beside me. I don't want to be separated from you again.'

'I can't think Rahim. I must ask my mother and father first.'

'Let's go now. If you want to change your clothes first, go ahead. I'll wait for you here.'

'I don't know what to do,' Malisa was still uncertain.

'Don't think any more, we'll just go.'

'Where's Rokiah?'

'I told you. She's in the car at the end of the road there.'

'I'd like to speak with her!' said Malisa.

'When you're ready, we'll go together. Then you can talk to her.'

'We must go to my parents' house first, alright?' Malisa was still in shock.

'Yes my love ... yes!'

Halim and Wati were in a lakeside restaurant.

'Wati, you're still silent...,' said Halim.

'Halim ... I'm so used to you. If you go from my life, I won't know how to be anymore.'

'Oh you can't get rid of me that easily.' Halim touched Wati's hand.

'I'm afraid!' said Wati.

'Afraid of what?'

'I'm afraid of the loneliness in this wide world!'

'Wati, if you were not married, I'd surely ask you to marry me,' said Halim smiling.

'It's strange! At the university, we moved in different circles. Now you already have two grown up children, and I have one. This is what is called life!'

'If it was possible I'd like to turn the cycle of history so that we could go back to being young as we were in the university and we could make a choice all over again....'

'Where would we put the three children?'

'You have a point there!'

'In the old days ... when I went out with you, I never felt guilty because my heart was sincere and honest. But now after Sofia said those things to me, I feel sinful,' said Wati.

'Don't trouble yourself over Sofia. What are we afraid of? We've not done anything.'

'Yes, we haven't done anything. But we're always together.'

'As long as we are not doing anything terrible, it's alright!'

Wati tapped her fingers on the tabletop and looked at Halim. 'Someone was spying on us this afternoon, did you realise that?'

'I had an idea I heard the door opening and closing. But I never really thought....'

'Yes ... someone was trying to come in. Whoever it was had a key. The key was left at the door when we were inside.'

'Perhaps it was a robber. Athough what does he want to steal? There's nothing much in the house!'

'Maybe Ahmad wanted to spy on us when he found out that I was going to the flat,' said Wati.

'We weren't doing anything....'

'Yes ... we weren't doing anything ... but at the time you were still wearing that towel!'

'Ah never mind ... it's not that you're not used to seeing me in a towel,' said Halim.

'Yes, that's right, it's Ahmad who's not used to seeing you in a towel in front of me.'

'I don't know, forget it. If Ahmad tells people, who'd believe him!' said Halim. 'You mentioned that Rahim was coming...?'

'Yes ... he came and went ... I don't know what he wanted to talk about, although it seemed urgent. I went back to the house earlier ... no one was there. That girl Malisa had already moved out while we were in Jakarta. She's staying with her cousin. Rahim's probably in Kaloi now!' said Wati.

'So how ... do you want to go back to your house or go to the night club or somewhere else?' asked Halim.

'I don't know Halim ... I'll go with you anywhere, but I don't want to be alone. I feel strange tonight. I feel that my life is lonely and empty. I feel sad....' Wati felt like crying, but she did not know why.

'Are you still thinking about Sofia?' asked Halim; he was playing with the ring on Wati's finger. Wati stared at the glass of lemonade in front of her.

'No ... not Sofia ... For the first time I feel I'm alone in this world. I feel that my life is meaningless.' Wati stared at the lights on the surface of the calm lake.

'Wati ... you're not alone. You have everything in the world. You're beautiful ... elegant ... you've got a good job ... a good husband. You've also been blessed with a son. What else do you seek?'

'Yes, Halim ... that's my question. I know there's something missing in my life. I feel a void in my soul that needs to be filled but I don't know what with.'

Wati reached for Halim's hand. She held the hand with both her hands and looked sadly into Halim's eyes. She kissed the rough fingers and placed them lovingly on her cheek.

'I know the day will come ... I must let you go from my life. I feel sad thinking of that day ... but I know I must face it.' Wati placed Halim's hand on the table. She looked at the lake again. The blank surface of the lake seemed to mirror an emptiness in Wati's soul.

'Why must we be separated?' asked Halim.

'Halim, as long as I didn't think about the feelings hidden in the depths of my heart, I was free ... in my actions ... to freely talk and joke without hesitation ... because I knew this heart iwa honest and sincere. But now I've realised... that there's something hidden in this heart. Knowing this, I cannot put aside those feelings and act as if they do not exist...'

'Wati, I don't want you to ever change or go away ... you bring so much to my life.''

'I must Halim ... we're not that young now ... both of us have families. We cannot think like students anymore. I need to let you go.'

'The reason?' asked Halim.

'The reason is that I've realised that you fill the emptiness in my life ... and I also realise that we're both married. With this realisation I feel guilty ... each time I look into your eyes, my heart beats faster seeing your smile.'

'What should we do, Wati?'

'That's the problem ... I'm between the devil and the deep blue sea.'

'Can you answer my question sincerely?' asked Halim, taking Wati's hand again.

Wati's heart was pounding again. She was afraid of questions like these that must be answered 'sincerely.' 'I'll try,' she said.

'Do you still love Rahim?'

Wati stared at Halim. She closed her eyes and her tears flowed. 'Yes, Halim ... I love Rahim with all my heart...,' said Wati.

Halim breathed in deeply. Slowly he let go of Wati's hand. Wati was not sure what Halim's feelings were but she had had given a sincere answer. She had stated the truth.

'Halim...!' Wati turned toward Halim.

'Hmm?' Halim looked at Wati. He wiped the tears on Wati's cheeks with the end of his fingers.

'Do you still love Sofia?'

Now Halim grasped Wati's hand again. 'As children we

promised to be together forever. Each time I looked at a lake this calm, I'd remember the times when we would go finishing; Sofia has become my flesh and blood, Wati. Now she's isolated herself but I'm still hoping she'd go back to loving me as she used to. I hope one day she'll forgive me.'

Wati held Halim's hand tightly. She smiled with relief. 'Thank you, Halim ... you're truly sincere. I appreciate you more now.'

'But Wati ... you give meaning to my life.'

'But that's not the issue now. Now I realise my mistake, I'm aware of it now. Because I love Sofia too much I was willing to set aside my dignity to take care of her husband so that he'd not be wild with other women. But I didn't realise by doing that I'd set a trap for myself. Now I've discovered why many women are easily attracted to you, Halim.'

Wati stopped for a moment. She looked at Halim again. He appeared as if he could not believe Wati's explanation.

'I'm burning now. I played with fire and now I'm the one who's burning,' said Wati.

'Wati, don't feel any regret. I never even once regretted our relationship.'

'But now I'm enemies with my best friend!'

'That's unintentional.'

'But, if I hadn't tried to help her, all this would never have happened!' said Wati.

'Don't think about the past. We can't do anything now!'

'Yes ... but I truly regret it!'

'Ah, don't think about it anymore ... let's go!' said Halim, touching Wati's shoulder.

Wati got up but her mind was far away. They walked toward the car.

'Are you leaving for Penang tomorrow?' asked Halim.

'Yes,' said Wati. She was lost in thought.

'How many days?'

'Three days...'

'Do you want me to go with you? I can go in the morning and come back at night.'

'No Halim ... I need to be away from you ... I need to think!'

'Yes ... I understand. But remember Wati ... I'll always be by your side, no matter what happens.'

Wati turned toward Halim. She stopped walking. Halim too stopped. She held Halim's hand.

'Thank you...,' said Wati. 'I'm afraid to face this world alone.'

15

'**HALIM**!' Wati had not expected Halim to be waiting for her at the airport. She was elated to see him.

'Why are you so amazed?' asked Halim, as he took the bag from Wati's hand. They walked toward Halim's car.

'I didn't think there was anyone waiting for me. I never told anyone when I'd be back,' said Wati.

'Like you once said ... everything you do, I know about it!' Halim gave her his mischievous smile.

'I don't believe it!' said Wati.

They marched through the busy airport. Wati looked radiantly happy. Strange, thought Halim. He had never seen Wati this happy. Whatever happened in Penang?

'You look extremely healthy, and well! You swam in the sea, didn't you?' asked Halim, turning as he walked.

'Yes ... I went to the beach each afternoon till sunset. I studied the natural beauty of the earth. I felt calmer, more peaceful. In those days, I continuously witnessed the beauty created by God. While I was in Penang I walked by the seaside ... I saw the rolling waves, I studied the broad sky, felt the peace spreading in my soul.'

'I can see your face is radiant.'

They reached the car. The door was opened. Wati climbed in. Halim put Wati's bag at the back of the car. He returned to the driver's seat and started the engine. He turned towards her: 'I'm happy to see you happy.'

The car sped to the main road. Halim turned right. He followed the road to the city.

'I never thought I could solve this mess in my mind,' said Wati, her eyes looking forward.

'Oh!' Halim did not quite understand.

'I understand now what is causing my empty feeling.'

'What?' Halim begin to feel nervous.

'I know now what's truly meaningful in my life.' Wati looked at the road in front of her, smiling.

'What?' Halim's heart was beating faster.

'My husband ... Rahim! Rahim is always not with me. We're separated by circumstances. He's in the village and I'm in the city.'

Halim took a deep breath. He knew that Wati had never forgotten Rahim, even though they were far apart.

'I'm happy to see you're no longer sad,' he said sincerely.

'We're so different. Our backgrounds are different. I'm from the city, he's from the village. Intellectually, we're also different ... not like you and me. Our attitudes are also different. He's quiet, serious ... I'm more open and social. Perhaps, this is why I'm so attracted to him,' explained Wati.

'Wati, you realise now what you're looking for in this life. You should not let things drift but take action!' said Halim, trying to remind her.

'Yes, I must do something. I'll go to Kaloi this very afternoon. I want to tell Rahim that I have been confused but no longer. I'll tell him that my life's empty without his presence each second. Maybe we need to shake things up. Maybe we need to live in a place situated between Kaloi and the city. He can drive to the east and I drive to the west,' said Wati, happy to arrive at a decision.

'Your plan sounds good. I hope we'll remain friends.'

Wati was silent, not daring to say anything. Halim stopped. The signal light was red.

'Where do you want me to take you?' asked Halim.

'I left my car at my house.'

'You want me to drive you to Kaloi?'

'No need ... thank you.'

The car moved forward. Wati smiled.

'Halim isn't angry that you're here at a party in my house?' asked Rahmah.

'I don't need a permit anymore if I want to go anywhere. He has a key, I have a key. Whoever wants to come back at whatever time ... it's up to us,' said Sofia washing the dishes.

'Well, your voice sounds really different,' said Rahmah, puzzled.

'I'm through with feeling jealous, now I'm just bored...,' said Sofia, with an edge.

'Bored ... what's the reason?' Rahmah placed the plates which she had brought from the living room on the kitchen table.

Sofia carried the dishes to the sink. 'I found out who the new woman is,' she said nonchalantly.

'Who?'

'My old friend?' said Sofia.

'Fatimawati?' Rahmah was shocked. 'Well, this is truly unexpected. How do you know?'

'I have proof!'

'Eh, proof can sometimes be misleading.'

'I found her lipstick in Halim's golf bag.'

'Maybe it's someone else's lipstick, or that girl's, Nora!'

'Also there's the cream she asked me to buy for her in Tokyo. That cream isn't sold here. She's the only one I know using the cream,'

'What's wrong with the cream and lipstick being in the golf bag?'.

'Didn't you tell me that found evidence back then that caused you to doubt your husband? Maybe you couldn't prove it for sure but experience told you the truth ... Put it this way... even though you're kind to Subardi ... Subardi would not keep your lipstick in his golf bag?' asked Sofia.

'Yes, you're right!' said Rahmah. 'So what did you do?'

'You think I'd stay quiet? It was time for me to explode! I had been patient far too long. What's worse is that Wati had pretended to sympathise with me! I telephoned her ... turned on her. I said what I wanted to say!' said Sofia, wiping her hand with a towel.

'That's good...'

'Well, it's time I left.' They heard Dr. Subardi's voice t the door and the conversation between Rahmah and Sofia stopped.

'Why're you leaving already?' asked Rahmah.

'Tomorrow I'm working very early,' said Dr. Subardi.

'Subardi, can I get a ride home? I pity Rahmah if she has to drive me. She's tired from all the cooking. And she has to clean up too. Earlier, I came with Datin Jamilah and *datuk* but they have all left. I stayed to help Rahmah with the dishes,' said Sofia.

'Are you really leaving?' asked Rahmah disappointed because she could not hear the rest of the story.

'Halim doesn't know that I'm here, does he?' asked Sofia.

'Ha! You said you were tired!'

Sofia smiled. Rahmah could easily catch what was on her mind.

'Thank you so much Rahmah.' Sofia shook hands with her friend.

Dr. Subardi was already waiting for Sofia outside. Sofia thanked Johari, Rahmah's husband who was outside, accompanying Dr. Subardi to his car.

'Don't go anywhere else, alright, Subardi!' Johari joked.

Sofia and Dr. Subardi smiled.

When they reached Sofia's home, Halim's car was in the garage. The gates were still opened. Maybe Halim had just arrived.

Seeing the gates opened, Dr. Subardi went straight into the compound, stopping his car behind Halim's. He turned off the engine. Although they lived close by, Dr. Subardi had never met Halim face-to-face. He was curious to meet Sofia's husband.

Halim heard the sound of a car driving in. He wondered where Sofia had been so late at night and felt rather uneasy. Sofia had never gone out without leaving a note or telling him beforehand. Previously, Sofia was just silent, but now she was rebellious, thought Halim. He heard the door close. Perhaps Rahmah and her husband drove Sofia home. Halim was familiar with Johari, but it had been a while since they last met. When he got to the door, he saw a white Volvo. He saw a man opening the door on Sofia's side. Sofia climbed out smiling. Her handbag dropped to the ground but was retrieved by the man.

Halim nervous feeling grew. This is why Sofia did not want to talk to me all this time, and does not want to entertain me, he thought. She already has a new heartthrob. She thinks she is still young and can behave as if she was a girl. She is someone's wife! Doesn't she realize it?

Dr. Subardi closed the door of the car as he accompanied Sofia to the door. As a doctor, he had a highly developed sense of responsibility and it was his habit to walk someone right up to the front door at such a late hour. Halim could not contain his impatience. His jealousy seized him suddenly and he opened the door.

Dr. Subardi, seeing Halim's face, understood that he was not welcome there. 'Good night, Sofia,' he said and walked quickly away.

Sofia was aware that Halim was watching her every move. At first she felt guilty for not having told Halim where she was going but when she remembered all of Halim's behaviour, she felt braver. She did not turn to her husband. She went straight to her room.

'Sofia!' She heard Halim's voice calling her.

Sofia stopped on the stairs and looked down. She knew Halim was angry but didn't feel afraid. She had done nothing wrong!

'Yes...,' she said. 'Do you want something to eat?'

Halim was quiet.

Sofia went down the stairs again. 'You want me to make something to drink?'

Halim looked squarely at Sofia, trying to suppress his anger. 'Who was that driving you home?'

'His name is Dr. Subardi. He lives in the white house

across the road. He works at the hospital in the city, and comes from Indonesia....'

'Enough! I don't want to hear about his background.'

Sofia was well aware that Halim was angry. Before, when Halim was that angry, Sofia was frightened. Now she did not feel afraid, she did not feel sad, she did not feel angry. In fact, if anything, she felt satisfied. Sofia did not run to her room and she did not cry as she often did... She took two to three steps, towards Halim whose seemed to be inwardly raging. She looked straight at him challengingly. 'You asked me who the man was. I only answered what you asked.' Her voice was calm, unwavering.

'Where have you been?'

'I was at Rahmah's house. She also invited you. They had a dinner party but you were late coming back. I had to help Rahmah in the kitchen. Joe telephoned later but you weren't home. There was nothing we could do,' said Sofia.

'Now you're going out with men whenever you like!' said Halim, forced to admit his feelings. He simply could not suppress his jealousy. He tried to hide it but failed.

'Don't tell me you feel jealous? I thought you didn't know the meaning of the word? Didn't you take me to Japan so that I'd learn to be like a Japanese wife, patient and obedient to the husband, and not jealous even though the husband is making out with another woman in front of her eyes or cheating with her best friend. I've now passed the test, I'm not jealous of your relationship with Wati You should be pleased that you've taught me to become stonehearted like you.'

'So you were really fooling around with that man while I wasn't at home?'

The Wife

Sofia did not answer. It was better to remain calm. She went straight to the kitchen and opened the refrigerator. She prepared two glasses of cold drinks. She could still hear Halim's voice shouting her name.

She went out again with a tray of cold drinks.

'You're so impatient! I was making these drinks, wasn't I?' Sofia sensed that Halim was really jealous. Now was the time for her to tell him a few things, thought Sofia.

Halim was sitting on the sofa. He appeared quieter in the face of Sofia's calmness. She placed the drinks on the table.

'What do you want to know? I can tell you everything. What's there to make a fuss about? Drink the lemonade first. Calm down and I'll answer your questions one by one,' said Sofia. She held out a glass of cold lemonade to Halim.

Halim took the glass without saying anything. He drank the lemonade all at once and then placed the empty glass back on the table.

'But...,' continued Sofia. 'You must also tell me everything that I want to know sincerely and honestly.'

Halim had never been questioned like this by Sofia. They had never calmly asked and answered each other's uestions honestly and sincerely without getting emotional.

Sofia drank a little of the lemonade. 'Alright ... what are you really angry about?' she asked him calmly. 'Is it because I went to Rahmah's house without your permission or is it because another man drove me home?' She put her glass on the table next to Halim's.

'I thought I was going to ask the questions,' said Halim.

'Oh...!' Sofia felt almost amused, but she tried to be serious. She knew now that Halim was truly jealous.

Halim looked at Sofa but he did not know what to ask.

Sofia was waiting.

'Alright ... what's your first question?' she asked.

'What's your relationship with that man?'.

'The man's name is Dr. Subardi....'

'I don't care what his name is!' Halim's voice rose.

'Get this ... if you raise your voice one more time ... I'll immediately go upstairs and will not answer any more questions,' said Sofia firmly.

Halim knew Sofia was serious.

'Alright, I'll ask again. What's your relationship with that... with Dr. Subardi?'

'If I answer in brief you might get the wrong idea. Let me tell you how I knew him. After that you decide what my relationship is with him.'

Halim began to worry.

'One afternoon, I was feeling anxious thinking about Nora, your ex-lover....' Halim appeared to want to protest but then kept silent. 'I was walking as usual on the road outside and I fainted and fell down in front of Dr. Subardi's house. I don't know how long I lay blacked out at the roadside. Fortunately I wasn't run over by a car -- though if I had been, there'd be no opportunity for you to torture me like this....' Sofia felt her chest tightening up. But she kept her tears from falling so that her weakness would not shown. She felt Halim touching her hand slowly. At first Sofia wanted to pull her hand away but she left it there.

'What happened next?' asked Halim. He was still holding Sofia's hand.

'Yes ... fortunately there was no car... It wasn't my time... Dr. Subardi was watering his plants and saw me lying at the roadside. He revived me. He also gave me medication. He

236

said my blood was thin and needed plenty of rest and that I should not worry too much. If I worried too much, it would endanger my life.'

She could feel Halim gripping her hand. Sofia allowed this.

'Even though Dr. Subardi always enquired about me and gave me medicine, I didn't take it. I prefer not to. What's the use of taking care of myself to live longer in this world filled with suffering. I've everything: a big house, a big car, a handsome husband with a good job; but my soul is suffering. I threw away all the medicine given by Dr. Subardi. This life has no meaning for me. You want to know about my relationship with Dr. Subardi. Tonight was the first time I was ever in his car. I was the one who was wrong. I asked him to give me a ride home because I had troubled Rahmah and Joe enough. They were already both tired. If you're still in doubt, ask Rahmah, Joe or Dr. Subardi himself,' said Sofia. She turned to Halim. She saw the painful look on Halim's face. He hadn't known about Sofia's illness, her suffering. Until now he had never fully understood the pain caused by his actions.

'Don't worry. Now I'm no longer jealous. The feelings of jealousy have died. I live because there's still life in me. My body still exists and my time hasn't come yet, that's all.' Sofia was trying to suppress her sorrow.

Halim buried his face in Sofia's shoulder. He could no longer suppress the sadness he was feeling in his heart.

'Sofia ... don't speak like that. I had no idea that you were suffering that much. I never knew,' said Halim. He held Sofia close. She closed her eyes and for the first time in front of him tears flowed down her cheeks.

'Sofia, forgive me, Sofia, I've hurt you. I've poisoned your life. You were ill and alone and suffering in silence,' said Halim.

'This world has no meaning for me. I don't need a house this big ... I don't need abundant wealth. I only desire your undivided love and if that cannot be given, I don't need anything else in this world,' said Sofia calmly.

'Sofia ... I promise!' Halim looked at Sofia.

Sofia placed her forefinger on Halim's lips.

'Don't promise. Don't. I was nearly killed by a promise. I'll continue to live without any promises from you.'

'Forgive me, Sofia,' said Halim, holding Sofia's hand, and looking into her eyes.

'You're not at fault.'

'But I want to hear you forgive me.'

'I have forgiven you long ago.'

'Will you love me again?' asked Halim.

'If my love gives meaning to your life, I'll give it willingly but....'

This time Halim closed Sofia's mouth with his fingers.

'Enough ... that's all I want to hear.' Halim held Sofia tightly. 'Oh Sofia, thank God, *alhamduli'llah*, you still love me. I was afraid earlier ... I thought that you had fallen in love with Dr. Subardi. I was afraid of losing you. My life would be empty without your love, Sofia.' Halim pulled her even closer.

Everything that Sofia had wanted to ask about Wati disappeared immediately. She no longer needed Halim's explanations. All she needed to know was that Halim still loved her. She only asked for Halim's love in this world.

Halim felt Sofia hugging him and caressing his neck. He realised that his wife loved him again.

The Wife

Wati drove her BMW as fast as she could. It had been a while since she went to Kaloi. Usually Rahim came to the city but this time Wati wanted to surprise Rahim. He probably hadn't remembered that it was their wedding anniversary and she'd bought a special gift for him in Penang.

Wati had made the decision to distance herself from Halim. She realised that in her attempt to rehabilitate him, she had trapped herself. Now Sofia had lost her best friend and would likely lose Halim too.

Nevertheless, Wati had started on a journey of change. She had tried to find out why she had this empty feeling. While in Penang, she finally time to think. She became closer to the beauty of nature created by Allah. Every evening before sunset, she walked along the beach, thankful for all that Allah had bestowed upon her. Wati had only just realised that everything she was looking for was already with her, only she had not been aware of it.

Her thoughts turned to her beloved husband. Circumstances had kept them far away from each other. Now Wati realised that she must return to Rahim and become a good wife. She was beginning to realise that in recent months she had placed more importance on another person's marriage than her own. And she had not even been successful in bringing back the happiness to that marriage -- in fact, she had nearly caused its demise.

Wati felt frightened when she thought of how close she had come to destroying her own marriage. She was determined to change her attitude. The thing she had been looking for was now completely clear. She realised that she needed Rahim, the husband she had ignored because she placed more importance on her career. Only Rahim could fill the emptiness in her heart.

Wati felt happy going back to Kaloi this time because she realised that the source of her happiness was there in that village. Rahim would surely be happy seeing her arrive. Wati turned her car toward Rahim's house. She saw that the Mercedes was not in the parking bay. Surely Rahim hadn't driven to the city to find her?

Wati parked her car, got out and reached for her handbag. A slow song was playing inside the house. There must be somebody home, thought Wati. She retrieved her luggage from the boot.

The front door of Rahim's house was opened. Wati placed her bags on the steps going up to the house. She was puzzled, wondering who had opened the door! Perhaps, Rahim had hired a maid now.

Someone was cooking in the kitchen but Wati was too exhausted to go there. Instead she brought her bags to the guestroom and then went straight to the bathroom to take a bath.

Malisa was busy frying bananas in the kitchen. She had heard a car driving in, went to open the door and went back to the kitchen. Usually, when Rahim got home, he would go straight to the kitchen to find Malisa.

Malisa brought tea and fried bananas to the living room. She could hear someone taking a shower in the guestroom. Perhaps Rahim was very tired and had gone straight up to shower. Malisa went back to the kitchen. She wanted to clear up while waiting for Rahim to come down.

Wati came out of the bathroom. She put on a new outfit which she had just bought. She knew that it was in Rahim's favourite colour. Rahim would surely be surprised to see her waiting at home.

In the living room tea had been served for two at the table. There were also fried bananas but no sugar, which was what Wati loved. She went to ktichen to look for it.

There was someone washing dishes with her back toward Wati....

'Where do you keep the sugar?' asked Wati.

Hearing Wati's voice, Malisa was startled. The plate in her hand dropped and broke. It was actually Wati, thought Malisa, who was frightened beyond words.

'Sorry ... I didn't mean to startle you!' said Wati.

Malisa turned toward Wati.

'Malisa! I didn't expect to see you here! You're not working today?'

'No, Wati!' Malisa answered hesitantly. Malisa did not know if Wati knew about the situation. She picked up the broken pieces of plate.

'Rokiah didn't come along?'

'No!'

'Where's Rahim?'

'I don't know.'

Wati shrugged and went back to the living room.

Malisa's entire body was shaking. She'd never expected Wati to come here. Oh Rahim! What should I do? Malisa did not want to face Wati like this. She must leave. Malisa remembered her neighbour, Mak Limah, who had once said, 'If you have any problem, I'm here to help.'

Malisa grabbed her handbag and left the house by the back door without Wati's knowledge.

Wati switched on the TV. Where could Rahim be, thought Wati. But never mind. Usually it was Rahim who had to wait. This time, it was Wati's turn.

A while later, she heard the Mercedes driving into the compound. Rahim saw the white BMW and realised that Wati was there. His heart was pounding. But what is there to be afraid of, thought Rahim. I am a man.

Wati heard Rahim's car approaching the house. She was certain that Rahim would be happy to see her. Wati got up and headed for the door to welcome Rahim home. She smiled as he climbed out of the car: 'Hello there!'

'Oh Wati! When did you arrive?' asked Rahim coming up to her

'Quite a while ago! Where have you come from?'

'Well, work of course! What else?' said Rahim. Wati took the file that he was carrying. Rahim looked at his wife and realised in that moment that he still loved her.

'Poor you, you look really tired. Would you like tea first? It's all ready. Or would you like me to run you a bath?' asked Wati.

Rahim was still quiet. Where was Malisa? Rahim went to the kitchen.Wati followed from behind, not knowing what Rahim was looking for. Where was Malisa? Rahim was beginning to worry. He headed toward the living room and then he went upstairs, to his room. Maybe Malisa was in the bedroom!

Wati followed Rahim upstairs. Wati knew Rahim was exhausted. When he was tired he usually did not speak much. She still held the file she had given him.

The Wife

Wati studied Rahim's clean and neat room. But this room seemed different than before, although she did not know what it was. After Rahim went to the bathroom, Wati noticed women's clothing hanging in the room; the clothes were not hers.

Rahim came out of the bathroom. He saw the look on Wati's face. Something must have happened between Malisa and Wati, thought Rahim. It must be!

'Whose clothes are these?' asked Wati. She opened the wardrobe, which was filled with women's clothing. She turned to Rahim, questioningly.

'Wati ... where's Malisa?' asked Rahim looking serious.

'She was in the kitchen earlier. What's wrong?'

'She's not in the kitchen. She's not anywhere...,' said Rahim dejectedly.

'You've not answered my question. Whose clothes are these?' asked Wati.

'You chased her out!' Rahim was accusing her.

'Who?' Wati was puzzled.

'My wife ... Malisa is my wife. You chased her out, didn't you?'

'Malisa is your wife? Rahim!!!' Wati yelled. 'I don't believe it!!' Wati screamed with all her might. She threw the files in her hand at Rahim's face. Out came a huge envelope ... with pictures of Wati and Halim embracing in Jakarta.

Wati was shocked to see the pictures strewn on the floor. She stopped screaming. Rahim watched silently as Wati bent down to retrieve the pictures with her in a swimming suit embracing Halim all wet in the swimming pool.

'I need to find Malisa!' said Rahim. 'I don't want to lose her. I've already lost you, Wati. I don't want Malisa to also disappear.'

'Rahim!' Wati screamed his name again. But Rahim had already gone downstairs.

The telephone rang. Rahim reached for it hastily.

'Hello! Rahim?' Malisa's voice could be heard, it sounded rather distant.

'Yes, my love ... Oh Malisa, where are you?'

'I thought that you might worry. I'm at Mak Limah's house. I'll wait until you settle the problem. I was afraid to face Wati,' said Malisa crying.

'Darling, don't cry. Thank God, you called, I was going mad. I thought you had run away. Oh Malisa!'

'No matter what happens, I'm still your wife ... I'll not run away....'

'Lisa, wait for me there ... don't go anywhere ... I'll worry if you go away. Wait for me alright!'

'Yes dear. I'll wait for you. Don't worry,' said Malisa, putting down the telephone.

Rahim turned. Wati was on the stair; she had heard everything that was said between him and Malisa.

'Wati...,' said Rahim, not knowing what to say.

'I never expected this. Oh Rahim!' Wati sobbed. 'I never thought Malisa would steal my husband!'

'It's not her fault, Wati. I needed a wife, not a lover. I needed a wife who would be by my side always. I wanted a life like other husbands who are cared for by their wives with love. I was tired of chasing after your shadow. I was tired of a life that was uncertain.'

Wati approached Rahim. His back was towards her. She embraced Rahim from behind. 'But Rahim, I had never stopped loving you. How could you have thrown away my love,' said Wati, as she whispered between sobs.

Rahim closed his eyes. He knew that he would weaken in Wati's embrace. Indeed his fury was beginning to subside.

'But you don't love me anymore. I even heard Halim asking you to marry him. How would a husband feel Wati, seeing his own wife with another man half naked?' said Rahim turning to look at her.

'So I was you spying on us that day!'

'Yes Wati, I saw it myself. I didn't hear it from others.'

'But we didn't do anything that day Rahim. Ask Halim ... if you don't believe me!'

'Wati ... think about it.' Rahim faced Wati who was still crying. He held her shoulders with both hands. He looked at her face. 'I drove many miles to see you. I had to cancel all my plans, but you made me wait in your office while you were with Halim. You think for yourself, if you were in that situation, how would you feel?' Rahim asked calmly.

'Rahim ... in spite of everything ... I love you, Rahim!' said Wati, embracing him. She buried her head in Rahim's shoulder.

'Wati....' Rahim caressed Wati's head trying to pacify her. Rahim knew no matter how angry he was with Wati, he still loved her. 'Wati ... I saw what I saw and at that moment, I believed you no longer loved me. I had to forget, I had to marry quickly so that my anger toward you would go away.'

'You're not fair, Rahim ... you're not fair,' Wati held Rahim closer and sobbed. 'I love you and today is our wedding anniversary. Is Malisa your special gift for me?'

Rahim suddenly remembered that he had been waiting for this day. This was a special night for the two of them. Rahim had bought a gift for his beloved wife two months before. The gift was still under the bed.

'Wati ... I didn't forget to buy a gift for our wedding anniversary.'

'I don't believe it...'

Wati let go of Rahim. She gave him an incredulous look.

'The gift is under the bed,' said Rahim.

'This means you really still love me?'

Rahim nodded. He wiped Wati's tears with his fingers.

'I was in Penang for the last three days,' she said. 'I really missed you. As soon as I arrived at the airport, I drove here. I wanted to tell you that I've realised my life is meaningless without you. I need you by my side.'

Now Rahim embraced Wati. Tears flowed down Rahim's cheeks.

Wati cupped Rahim's face with her two hands. 'Why are you crying Rahim ... why?' asked Wati. She wiped the tears that were flowing down Rahim's cheeks. She had never seen Rahim cry.

'Wati, why do you say these things now? Why only now?' asked Rahim.

Wati did not understand. She looked at Rahim questioningly.

'Malisa is now my responsibility, Wati!'

'Rahim ... how could you have married her ...' Wati released herself from Rahim's arms. She sat in a chair.

Rahim sat beside Wati.

'Wati, what about you and Halim? How could you be so intimate with him?'

'Yes, Rahim ... we may appear intimate, but actually we're not. I left him because I still love you. I didn't want to spoil our love.'

Rahim held his head in his hands.'I didn't realize, I didn't know… But now… Everything's too late…'

'If you really want to, you could find a way.'

'What are you implying?'

'You can divorce her!'

'Wati! She has done nothing wrong!' Rahim objected.

'If that's the case … you can divorce me. My mistakes are enough for you to divorce me. I won't accept you having another wife!'

'But Wati … don't you love me?' asked Rahim, holding Wati's shoulders, looking squarely into her eyes.

'That's another matter!' said Wati looking elsewhere.

'Love and marriage are the same matter … not separate matters. I don't want to divorce you because I love you … and you love me.'

'But I don't love you anymore!'

'I don't believe you. You just told me how much you loved me.'

'But if you give more significance to Malisa … take her. Just leave me.'

'No Wati. I love you!'

'But you also love Malisa….'

'Yes, I don't want to break her heart. She's very sincere!'

'I don't want to share you with another woman. You must choose either one of us: Malisa or me,' said Wati, this time firmly.

'I will not divorce Malisa. She hasn't done anything wrong,' said Rahim seriously.

'I'm the guilty one. So, just divorce me.'

'Even if you were wrong, I still love you. I'll not let you go.'

'You're not being fair!'

'Forgive me Wati … this wasn't what I wanted.'

'If it wasn't what you wanted, it wouldn't have happened!'

'Yes, I married Malisa because I thought you didn't love me anymore. But now I know that you do, I'll never let you go,' said Rahim.

'I regret telling you. It would have been better for you to think that I no longer love you.' Wati clasped her hands together. 'Forgive me, Rahim. If you have made your decision, be happy. Let me suffer. Let me be the lonely one without you. I'd just realised that you're the one who gives meaning to my life. But the realisation was too late. You didn't give me any chance to explain. If you love me, one day you'll send me a divorce letter.'

'Wati ... you're still my wife.' Rahim tired to plead again.

Wati rose. She took her bags from the living room. She opened the door.

'Don't go Wati ... it's already dark.'

'I no longer care what happens to me. I don't care anymore!' said Wati, going out.

Rahim followed her from behind. 'Wati!'

'You take care of your wife, Rahim. I pray that you'll divorce me one day.'

Wati opened the car door.

Rahim took Wati's hand.

'Wati, will you answer my question again, but sincerely?'

'Yes ... what is it?' Wati turned, looking at Rahim dejectedly.

'I want to hear it one more time! Do you love me?'

Wati felt weak in the knees. She wanted to hold Rahim again. She wanted to cry on his shoulders, but she steeled her heart and climbed into the car. She started the engine. In the dim of the night, Rahim saw Wati nodding, her tears flowing.

The Wife

'Yes, no matter what happens!' said Wati, in her sobs.

She did not wait for Rahim's response. She could no longer bear it. Her heart was broken, crushed, melted. She did not want to see Rahim's face. She reversed the car a little. After that Wati pressed the accelerator with all her might.

Wati wanted to ask Rahim the same question. But what was the use? What use was a love that is divided? What was it for? She drove on through the darkness of the night. She had lost everything. Her life felt empty without her true friend ... her beloved husband. Her life felt truly lonely. In the quietness of Kampung Kaloi, only the street lights were switched on here and there.

Where to? Wati asked herself. Where should I go? Wati was stumbling in the darkness of life. Wati was floating in a shoreless ocean ... She was without anything to hold on to, without guidance, all alone and so lonely.

www.makedopublishing.com

New Writing From Asia